Lockers Speak

Voices from America's Youth

Brenda Mahler

The characters and events portrayed in this book are fictitious. Any similarity to real persons, living or dead, is coincidental and not intended by the author.

ISBN-13: 9798508058562

Cover design by: Sierra Gil
Printed in the United States of America

We can learn to see each other and see ourselves in each other and recognize that human beings are more alike than we are unalike.

MAYA ANGELOU

Table of Contents

Prologue

As she walks by locker 623, she notices the door is hanging open. With the palm of her hand, she reaches out to push it shut and continues walking. Metal hits metal causing the door to swing back open without the familiar click that acknowledges it has latched. Upon closer inspection and a slight jiggle, a folded slip of paper falls to the floor, a simple system that allows for easy access without a combination. To the untrained eye, it is just a piece of paper; to high school students, it's a shortcut, a quick and easy access; to her eye, an administrator, it's an invitation to theft, vandalism, and bullying.

This locker needs some TLC by a custodian before a new tenant arrives in August. A mirror adheres to the interior, somewhat askew, probably from the constant slamming and jarring. The bottom shelf houses a battalion of ants extracting nourishment from the unidentifiable substance coating the surface. She writes a note to the janitor on the notepad in her hand, records the locker number and scribbles her name, Mrs. Smith.

Though no backpacks, purses, or personal items exist, evidence of the experiences that occurred here during the school year remain. A name carved into the metal on the right-side wall surrounded by a heart provides only clues to the identity of a crush turned true love then faded as quickly as the weather changes. Only the three letters, m-a-n, remain distinguishable because a heartbroken teen scratched out the other letters leaving only the original grey metal.

Names run through her mind of possibilities, maybe Luis Guzman. Rumors spread that girls craved his company, and his name was synonymous with the word player. His sister Ava might be the lost love. Those two both seemed to attract the interest of drooling peers. Maybe the Tilman boy, Morgan, but he never seemed too interested in girls or did they show much interest in him. Surely not Jack Pitman, the ultimate loner. The only emotion he ever showed consisted of contempt towards adults. Mrs. Smith shakes her head assaulted by the students' names and attitudes that flash through her mind.

Besides their lunches and books students carry their experiences, concerns, past, present, and future. Everything, good and bad, bits and pieces of life crammed into these lockers. Some students expose their life like pictures pasted on the locker walls while others buried any evidence of their identity under piles of papers, inside notebooks, folded, stapled, and abandoned beneath leftovers from long ago lunches and locked behind metal doors.

Not daring a closer inspection, she moves on thinking about the stories these cubicles might reveal, and the glimpse into teenage minds they would expose if they could speak.

It's the end of yet another school year. The empty, ravished halls reflect the lives of the teens beginning summer break. They have raced out thinking of pool parties, skateboard parks, and love interests. Their thoughts, like the teachers and hers, race from what they could do, to what they might do, but never settle on what they will do during the two months of free time.

This is a day of celebration because nobody is assigning homework or asking questions with vague answers. For the students and adults, the unknown sparks excitement like lightning hitting a power line. Excitement for the possibilities and the knowledge that the "must do" list is now shorter than yesterday. But under the immediate excitement lives anxiety because for many mixed with the fun plans is isolation, emptiness, and the unknown, and for some will emerge bad choices, unexpected consequences, and irrevocable decisions.

Her foot kicks a folded 2-inch triangle. The once smooth paper looks worn as it lays creased and folded with the flaps tucked under to secure the message inside. Out of curiosity she unwraps the note, reads the contents to discover a love letter. Through a series of loopy letters, acronyms, and icons, a message reveals a covert meeting planned for later at the water tower. Teardrops mark the edges of the page, each letter i is dotted with a heart, and XOXOXOs run along the bottom of the page. Instead of returning it to the trash piles on the floor that have accumulated during the locker clean-out, she lets it drift into an already full trashcan wondering what other information lies among the torn papers, discarded notebooks, and broken pencils.

Leaning to the left, she avoids an open locker door. The recently vacated cubicles trigger memories, anecdotes students were screaming to share but were protecting from discovery. As a principal, she witnesses students from a rare vantage point, youth growing up in modern society, a culture different from their parents', striving to define their world yet becoming human mirrors reflecting a changing world.

Their lives reveal problems exclusive to their generation, issues enhanced by the 24/7 news cycle and social media. Their thoughts impart wisdom; what they don't say tells a different story. Like puzzle pieces, when all the stories unite, a picture begins to emerge. Whether the stories are accurate or flawed becomes unimportant because they are believed, rumored, embellished and are now gospel.

Seldom does a person share the whole story because everyone is influenced by their singular perspective. However, the lockers before her whispering stories reflect the faces of the inhabitants whose eyes communicate. Their past limited, the future unclear, their stories flourish - alive and developing. If the lockers could speak, they would expose thoughts of the students who make decisions for the future.

Over the summer, many new chapters will be written. Mrs. Smith will have a lot to catch up on. For now, she continues to stroll down the hall, stopping occasionally to talk to a teacher, pick up a discarded book needing to be shelved, or make a note of a needed repair. All the while, whispering voices scream from the lockers.

Grayson Tannanbaum

Dad says,
All the men in our family are leaders
Our family tree goes back to Honest Abe
One year on student council will
    give me experience
    look good on my resume
    set me above the others

Dad says public school isn't challenging
So independent study for me
Home school and a tutor

Dad says
Ignore distractions
Work on a computer
Challenge my mind
No men in our family are followers
All are leaders

When asked questions,
I give answers

When I ask,
"How can I lead at home
from behind a computer?"

Dad's eyebrows raise
His words are silent

Emma Rose Reece

This year was awesome!
Being with Grayson makes me so happy
He knows how to treat a lady.
Mom and Dad say I am too young to get serious
but this is true love
They just don't remember what it is like
to care about someone this much
In my heart, I know
we will be together forever

Grayson is totally awesome!!
Next year, he will be homeschooled
What a hassle! Ugh!
His dad says,
"My son will be prepared for the real world of business."

We will talk everyday - Text, Instagram, Twitter
He will be as close as my pocket
and we will see each other
whenever we can

Today was so awesome!
Everybody was getting autographs
Some girls were crying
Really?
We will be together almost everyday
Softball camp starts Monday morning
We meet at Pizza Hut tonight
then off to Maddie's party.
Some of the guys are planning to drop by

Grayson didn't have time to sign my yearbook
Girls surrounded him all day
Since I am his gal,
I am saving the whole last page
just for him

Katie DeCroix

Boys can be so mean!
Did you hear
what Donny said about Joey?

Someone told me
he called him a retard.
I told mom
She said I can't hang with him anymore
Like I would want to.
What a creep!

Joey works so hard to fit in
It's just that people don't understand him
They don't even try!
He's smart you know
He can do math in his head
better than me
Kids think he's stuck-up because he's so smart
He's my brother so
I love him

But he never looks up from the ground
or makes eye contact - ever
When he mumbles, it is hard to hear
and he talks so fast his words run together,
Everyone should try harder
I just wish he didn't repeat everything
Multiple times
All the time

In the halls, Joey runs into people
He smiles and walks right into them
It is so embarrassing
Sometimes,
I just look the other way because I
wouldn't know what to say when they laugh
Kids would like him better
if he wasn't so annoying

Ben Thaire

I walk through the halls
    "Hi, Bennie"
    "Yo, Ben"
Someone nods recognition
I nod
Girls stare
Some seem to accuse;
Others look like they own me
I avoid eye contact

On the field, I am part of a team
My number is greeted with chants
    "Been there! Done That!"
    "Ben Thaire! Done That!"
At that moment
I am important

Joey's smile is sincere,
Inviting and friendly
I want to check in with him
He calls me his peer tutor
I call him my friend

Joey DeCroix

i like skool learning is fun
kids smile and laugh
the halls are crowded
when i
solve math problems
kids write down the ansers
donny winked at me
his friends smiled
i like skool i like to share
it makes people smile
ms. Thompson said,
the inverse of
$f(x) = 2x+3$ is $f-1(y) = (y-3)/2$
that made me smile
she
is a good teacher
ben is funny
everyone says
ben their don tat

Matt Colt

I am not ALWAYS right
Just usually
So why should I listen to Katie
She is just a girl
A smart girl – maybe -
But a girl

She wants to go out with me
but can't accept the fact that
I called it right
Joey is slow in the head
Everyone thinks it
What's so bad about saying it aloud?

It's not like it hurts his feelings
Yeah, he has feelings but he's
a little short in the brain department
Katie, she has brains but
She's not rational, not logical
She's an emotional thinker

After her refusing to go out- twice,
I'm not asking again
She'll see what a mistake she's making
She'll come pleading to me
I'll accept her apology

Sarah Sweet

I wish more classes are with friends
The only time I get out of the dungeon
is for electives and lunch
I go to special classes

Why are they in the basement?
They don't make me feel special - just stupid
Lunch is fun but frustrating
I am always catching up on the news

Rumor is Kirsten moved to attend a private school
But Emma says her parents sent her to a relative in Chicago
Donny is already eating lunch with that new girl
I'll have to ask Barb

Aubree says she is going to Europe this summer
I thought she had to take summer school
Sometimes I doubt what she says
but who really cares?

Grayson is going to be homeschooled
Emma Rose says she doesn't care 'cuz they'll talk daily
But I saw her crying in the bathroom
How long can that relationship last?

Well, some things stay constant –
I will be in the basement again next year
but for the summer I am part of the action
I'll hear the news firsthand
on Instagram

Aubree Topol

My parents are happy – together for 26 years
My brother is on a mission
My sister is married

I have a puppy – a Shiatsu
I have a 4.0 GPA as a junior
I have a boyfriend in college

Our grandparents live in Arizona
Our new house will be done next month
Our vacation is scheduled in Europe

Friends adore me
Teachers admire my abilities
Parents know I am a positive influence

I am a good girl
In a great school
From a respected family

Naomi Naus

I live with my grandma
She is a great support and a terrific listener
Sometimes we don't have a lot of money, but we get by
Grams says each day is a new adventure
"Make it happen"

With her encouragement, I go to school
play sports, work on the off seasons
Sometimes, when there is free time
see a movie or go for a walk

I don't tell everyone my parents are happily married
like Aubree, who swears hers never argue
We know they live in opposite ends of that ginormous house
She wouldn't know the truth if it stared in the eyes

Nobody ever promised life would be easy
Nobody made any promises at all; I'm realistic
I just take one day at a time
Set a goal and make it happen

Donny Smith

Kirsten's mom says she is visiting relatives in Chicago
Something about studying at a special school of art
I miss her attention but with her gone
the problem is gone
Life goes on

Katie's mom says she is too young to date
They let her go to the dance with someone
But only because it was school related
Now,
she doesn't respond to my texts

Steady girlfriends can be a drag anyway
They weigh a guy down, limit opportunities
I think I'll just play the field; see what happens
Things always happen,
if you know what I mean

All the guys are hangin' at a party this weekend
It's at the church but that doesn't mean we are Jesus Freaks
There's a girl, Mary. She's cute and I kinda like her
I will try to get to know her –
like in the Biblical way

Pratt Brothers (Derrick and John)

We share a locker

We share a life

Yeah, dad taught us one for all

All for one

I start the joke

I finish for the laugh

Together we walk the halls

As a team – best friends

PBJ

Quite a clever moniker

Pratt Brothers

Jonah and John

Together forever

Forever together

Get it?

Got it!

Good.

Jett Madden

Kirsten was my first playmate
My first friend
Girlfriend, Kiss, Wife, Love
I wish for our imaginary life as kids

When we got older, we stopped dressing up
and pretending to be married
She smiled and said she loved me
but added, "You're like my older brother."

From the first day, we ventured into high school,
She was noticed, a topic of conversation
So naïve, so sweet, so ready for adventure
Inexperienced, Fresh, Exploitable

She confided in me her love for Donny Smith
I watched her stare and smile before he knew she existed
She dressed and giggled to get his attention
Over time, attention she got

Donny noticed her;
He leered at her body as a prize to win
I appreciated her;
I worshiped her like a holy temple
Where other boys saw sexy legs, a slender waist, full breasts,
I saw a beautiful, vulnerable young lady needing to be held

I sat with her when she took the first test,
the second, then the third
I watched her eyes light up with excitement
when she spoke of telling Donny the news

I held her after he asked,
"Can the test be wrong?"
"Are you sure it's mine?"
I held her tight

Now, I scream,
"It should me mine. She should be mine!"

Kirsten Kelly

Mom doesn't want my reputation soiled
So, I am off to visit relatives

Visit? Is a prison sentence a visit?
This is cruel and unusual punishment, Ugh!

I just LOVE living with Aunt Helen
And her sappy, puritan family

They don't even have cable TV
A night out is eating a sandwich at Subway

Like it didn't hurt enough when I lost the baby
Now, I can't even talk to Donny

He must be heartsick. I miss him to death
Didn't even get to say goodbye

My family's coming next week
They will break the boredom but . . .

Their anxiety, my regret, and a lot of blame
Create a combustible equation

Barb Kelly

Saturday, I am going to the mall to buy that floral mini skirt
maybe some strappy wedges
My new highlights will scream, "I'm here."
Oh, this is going to be a super summer

Tonight, Sarah and Karli are going to sleep over
Mom agreed to drive us after breakfast
She is kinda sad lately, and I feel kinda bad for her
but the attention is kinda nice for a change

Life is sure different with Kirsten living at Aunt Helen's
Sometimes it's hard to be a twin
Especially when she is (no, was) perfect
Well, she isn't the favorite child anymore

Kirsten wasn't a virgin before Donny; I wonder if Mom knows
She watches me like a hawk
She will probably never let me date again
It wasn't me who embarrassed the family

Hmm, maybe we could have
Pizza after shopping.
Then maybe a movie
Life is good

Karlie Bruins

I don't understand!
She says she wants to help
Then she yells at me
You would think a teacher would like kids
It's not my fault

Most of the time I work hard
But then the paper has a low grade
Returned with red marks:
Sp
Awk
V.T.
Whatever those mean

Then Mom yells too,
"Try harder"
Like I go to class and don't try
How can I try when I'm sittin' in the hall?

The teacher accused me of writing on the poster
She does smell, but I didn't write it
They say it's recorded on video
Teachers sure make it hard to like school

Mary Scully

I have seminary fourth period
I wonder if Sofia wants to go out for lunch
We've been studying the Sins of the Flesh
Let's drive to lunch
We can ride with one of the Pratt boys
Maybe Donny drove today

Donny? He's my boyfriend
He always goes to lunch with us
Donny is a really good Christian
He works at McD's and gets us free food
What do you think?
Taco Time or Mack Attack?

We can be back in time for class. If not,
we will tell Brother Tom we ran out of gas
I think Sofia would love to hang with us
Who wouldn't?
There are some really great guys
I can hook her up with someone cute

We are so blessed to be friends
Oh yeah, our church group is having a party
Do you know Jesus as your personal Savior?
We are going to have so much fun

Sofia Ochoa

I love hanging with Mary and her friends
but I really don't like their church
They all talk holier than thou but don't act christiany
I guess there's nothing wrong with having a little fun

I don't know if I have the heart to tell her
Donny is not her boyfriend
According to him
He is "unattached"
He used that exact word
when his hand was on my thigh

I have to take an invite when I can 'cuz mom's so strict
She makes such a big deal when teachers take my phone
as if everybody doesn't text
Teachers just pick on me

I texted Francis,
"I have them for you,"
Her mom automatically assumed
the worst. What happened to
innocent until proven guilty?
I could have been talking about anything

Now Francis is mad at me
Says it is my fault that she is in trouble. Really?
Mom searches my phone because her mom suggested it
It seems to me that she caused the trouble

Well, if nothing better comes up, to church I go
At least mom can't complain about that
Besides Donny's supposed to be there
Halleluiah!

Francis Obray

We're outta here; let's have some fun
Thank god Mom believed me
When she found that note
I thought my summer was ruined
or worse, my life, if I couldn't hangout
I would be exiled in August when school starts

Ever since Mom found those two in my backpack,
She randomly searches my things
I told her they belong to Sofia
Now she's reading every slip of paper
I guess my phone too
I will have to be more careful

I can't believe Sofia could be so stupid
She claims she didn't do anything wrong
but what could Mom think when she read,
"Do you still want them?"
Kittens?
Colored pencils?

Mom has no right!
Where does she get off?
A little privacy wouldn't be too much to ask
Thanks to quick thinking,
"Movie tickets, Mom."
I sweetly replied even though I was seething

Well, it could have been worse
than starting vacation with a movie
I just wish we weren't seeing that stupid cartoon
So much for quick thinking
I also wish she hadn't replied in that sickening
sweet voice, "I'll drive you."

Maddie Chung

The yearbook has my name spelled wrong!
But it has six pictures of me!!
I wonder if anyone notices how my blue shirt
shows off my eyes

I am so glad our softball team made the playoffs
My position is backup right field so there's limited playing time
but I am decent, and the trip was awesome
A whole page of the yearbook is devoted to the tournament

The band trip, let me tell you, IT WAS WONDERFUL
Grayson kissed me (on the lips) in the back of the bus
but then the teacher assigned seats
Girls up front- boys in the back

Last week I saw a movie with Donny Smith
Well, we went to a movie and saw the first part
but then it ended, and the lights came up
When we left he said, "I'll catch you later."

He wants to see me again!

Can't wait to read my yearbook at home
Everyone signed it, and some wrote notes
Some of the boys are really gross
Why do they write that stuff? Mom is going to be mad!

Ethan Gram

My parents buy me only the best clothes
because as they say,
"Everybody loves a sharp dressed man."
An image is created; it doesn't just happen

The first day of high school was my beginning
I remember walking through the halls
establishing my turf
scoping out the hot spots

My path through the halls follows a pattern-
past the office, around the cafeteria
through senior hall to check out the chicks
loitering outside the library to glare at the geeks
down the stairs toward the gym to sneer at the jocks
out the back doors and again back past the office

Sometimes the path veers slightly to confuse anyone watching
Routines instill comfort and hide my discomfort
My path isn't planned to go in circles,
but I remember
when I realized it does

Now as the year comes to an end, I will be remembered
as the cool dude-
Smooth talker
Perfect attendance
Nobody needs to know
I earned no credits

Mary Schneider

Jessica and I are going to the waterpark
Everyday
Everyone is going to live there

We can ride the city bus
then walk two blocks
We agreed

My new swimsuit is - Oo La La
sexy
curves in all the right places
Those right places toned and tanned

Randy says we can be friends
with benefits
if I wear it very often
My face flushed
I hope he didn't notice
I am not a child

Colleen's going to hang with us
if she stops laughing like a donkey
She wants to bring her little brother
Like duh – No!
I want to be a guy magnet
not a repellant

Coach Douglas schedules daily practices
but the guys can't practice all the time
and when they're not on the field
let the games begin

Randy Otto

Girlfriends are an anchor around a man's neck
I like to play the field
No one girl has ever trapped me
If (big if) I want a girl
all I'll have do is snap my fingers
Short term relationships suit me

You'll never see me hang with Jo
He's a little light in the loafers
We used to hang
He made summer fun: fishing, bikes, playn' ball
but then he wanted to confide in me
I don't want to know his shit

Why'd he turn out queer? No,
he has a right to his own – whatever –
but I ain't gonna hang out with him
I know it's not contagious
but you know,
guilt by association

Not gonna let anyone call me Tinkerbell
Ramsey says he remembers when we were close friends
Emphasis on close. Hell, NO!
Gonna see if Mary wants to hang
I hear she has a pass to the swim park
It never hurts to have a girl around

Jo Fields

I hate being separated from the others
It sucks
Dressing down in the nurses' bathroom
is still better than the locker room
Kids are so mean

My gym shoes were stolen
They called me names
When Cole tripped me, everyone smirked
No, I didn't hear them
They think they're so cool

The worst was the accusations
I never did what they said
and them calling me Josephine
My counselor says they are covering
their insecurities through humor

Why do THEY need to accept
MY differences?
It's not their business, and it's not funny
They can ignore me, pretend I don't exist
Whatever – just leave me alone

Cole Nicholas

I didn't trip Jo
He isn't real sure footed –
Sure about anything
Some might even say he's conflicted
He just happened to walk where
I had extended my legs
What can I say?

Jo complains all the time
Says, people pick on him
Seems like a choice to me
Get it?
Choice?
If he didn't stand out so much
nobody would bother him
He should at least try to blend in

I've been told I have issues with change
but why change what works?
Uncle Tom says everything was better
back when white was white
black was black
and grey was a color
not a shade or a mix of two other colors

Something is wrong
in a world with no absolutes
For instance,
teachers all interpret rules differently

Mrs. Casey lets us use cell phones for math
If we snap a pic or post on Snap Chat, who cares?

Mr. Pete tells us to put the phones away
But Mr. Magoo doesn't see what's in front of his face

And if old lady Pierce sees a phone, she owns it
How can that be fair? Taking what is mine?

How is a guy supposed to know the rules
let alone remember the expectations?
There should be one way, the right way
It's so confusing. Uncle Tom says,
"Right used to be right.
Wrong used to be wrong."
What is wrong with this world?

Jessica Delaney

People say they care
then cause trouble
If they really care
they will leave me alone
I am just tired
Tired of the questions

Nothing
Nothing is wrong
Everyone keeps asking
The answer is always the same
Nothing

I told that nosey girl
my cat scratched me
She told the counselor
who called my parents

They already know
It's nobody's business
The counselor wants to talk – again

Nothing is wrong
Nothing.
Geez

Len Ma

Daddy is gone
He didn't die
That might be easier
We lost him to the world

It was a shock to watch him
walk away from our life,
his childhood sweetheart and daughter
The truth hurt; there was another woman

Mom's absence was subtle
She remained in the room
Nonexistent. Drinking non-nourishing
sustenance that camouflaged as courage

Mom said she felt hurt, unwanted
never acknowledging my numbness
When life seems hopeless
a child stops feeling

Dad never said anything because
he never visited, until he did
Then, they both made promises
as near perfect as imaginable

One week with Mom – one with Dad
When the world reached out again,
Daddy taught me forever is short
Love is conditional

Mom remarried a great guy
I welcomed the new man into the house
When my brother was born,
the walls warmed into a home

We are a family of four.
three adults and an infant
At thirteen,
my childhood is over

Colleen Knight

Thank god for a cellphone
Otherwise, I am locked at home,
all summer,
babysitting my little brother
and everyone will forget I exist

This year I will be in their minds
'cuz, I make things happen
Rolfe LOVES the pics I send
I even notice guys checking me out
when I walk down the hall

When Rolfe goes swimming,
I will put on my new bikini,
send pictures of me with a pouty face
He doesn't need to know
I am beside a plastic kiddie pool

When Gunnar and he are at the mall
I'll Snapchat a pic of myself
at a good angle wearing the sundress
with the sunflower and low neckline
that I ordered online

When they are at Burger Den,
they'll see me at a family bar-b-que
The fam will be cropped out
The focus will be on my sulky eyes,
painted lips and a strawberry

My body may not be beside them
maybe not physically
but it will be on their minds
until we meet again

Gunnar Hall

Yeah,
I won't graduate
Ha!
Never wanted to go
to college

Like it really matters
in the course of my life

Yeah, I don't really care

Justin French

At a young age, I was diagnosed
Told competitive sports were out of the question
Indefinitely
Too dangerous – especially contact sports
An inner ear problem made my balance unsure
I was destined to be a sideliner

However, at a young age, I caught the bug
Football, golf, tennis, soccer, baseball
You name it;
I love it
Since sports define me, I found other ways
to be one of the guys, involved with the team

I ref for my brother's little league
Attend all the area events
Everything
Volunteer as assistant coach at my high school
Water boy really, but I am on the field
A part of the action and a member of the team

Is it ideal?
No
Would I like to play?
You bet
I take what I can get

Rolfe King

Football is my future
They tried to sideline me the last game
even though SHE sent them to ME

The principal claims the pictures on my phone are illegal
Mom says they are making a mountain out of a molehill
"Boys will be boys," is Dad's mantra

Pull me out of the championship game
Really!?
He must be kidding. Get a life!

Our lawyer made him change his mind
I guess Dad is right
There is nothing that money can't buy

They wouldn't have won that game without me –
Sacked the QB 3 times!
Colleges are fighting over me

No deal is sealed yet
Boone, Ramsey, and Wyatt have all closed a deal
Scouts will call next week
My day is coming
My old man says it will happen
I will be the third generation at Dad's alma mater

I don't know what the big deal is anyways
Nobody cares about my discipline file
It's about throwing a ball and tackling

Alex Mench

I don't really understand why
my answers are wrong
I fill in all the blanks
provide answers

I get help from a peer mentor
I don't mind the extra work
The teacher doesn't single me out
as much

Everything was going pretty good

Until Rolfe depantsed me
Now, kids are being mean
Boone says, I'm the butt of the joke
I don't get it
I don't like school anymore

Robert Boone

I can't wait to get out of this place!
Kids are such pigs
Can't trust any of 'em

When I tripped on the bus, kids laughed
Somebody put that stuff in the aisle on purpose
It's not funny!

They hit me in PE, spit on my sandwich
wrote on my neck with a permanent marker
Lewis called me a loser

David would rather fit in than be my friend
He ignores me and acts like nothing's happening

Buck told Dad about Lewis, Kellan and Tom
Dad is pissed! Not about what happened
but that a Boone is a target
"No son of mine is gonna get treated that way."
He called the school, yelling, and threatening
"We aren't taking this crap!"

Like a phone call will make a difference

I will miss not having Buck around next year
but having him away at college will
make life easier with less pressure
No one to live up to
I will never fill his shoes but
maybe I'll learn to walk in my own

Buck Boone

Ramsey Stuart is my buddy
I wanted to kill Gunnar
when he called us a bromance
When was having a guy-friend a crime?
Gunnar's just mad because he won't graduate
What a loser!
Even Mench is going to graduate

Football is my existence
Fun to be had on the field,
during practice, at games,
in the locker room
Man did I laugh when Rolfe pulled
Mench's pants down to his ankles
Everyone thought it was funny

That pic of Colleen is NICE
She's the bomb
Easy to talk to
but clingy. I dated her once
Shouldn't girls wait for the guy to call?
Maybe later, I will text her
She could use a friend

Leaving Robert will be rough – for both of us
But a relief to dump that responsibility
He is my little brother but such a dweeb
I can't really blame Lewis and Kellen
Dad says blood is thicker than water
He sure expects a lot

David Clark

When does a compliment become an insult?

It's not ok to say black
It's called discrimination
Racism
But yet, ginger is ok?

I have something they will never have
I am an original
I share a nod of acknowledgement with
the other three redheads in the building

I felt bad when they bullied Robert
but I didn't want to draw attention to myself
Why have both of us suffering?
I can still support him; he is my friend

Vicky Lee

We've been hangin' out all spring
Started boating the first hot day
Well, not exactly hot - warm
I am the youngest in the group, a freshman
The guys are all seniors

There is no way I am not going to
accept a challenge

All eyes were on me
which increases the pleasure
I climbed on the wakeboard,
knowing it was not going to end well
Pumping adrenaline provided courage
and I won't deny I was a little buzzed
which also bolstered my bravery,
at least camouflaged the
stupidity of my actions

I remember Buck shouting
"Cross the wake!"
Why not?
I remember I was in the air,
the board above me
I remember the board struck my head
when I smacked the water

Waking up in the emergency room
alone was terrifying
Nobody I knew was around
but I felt better when the nurse
confirmed no broken bones
Concussion
Nothing I couldn't deal with
Seems weird that everyone left

This is just the beginning of summer
Let's party!

Wyatt Adams

A guy's gotta stay true blue to his buddies
even when they see the world a little skewed
but after all we've been through
it's one for all and all for one

I do wish Boone and Ramsey would try a little harder,
especially when schoolwork comes so easy
Accomplishments on the field can only take a guy so far
They could have it all without breaking a sweat

Man, I hate Tannanbaum and his holier than thou attitude
What I'd give to have his money, looks, and brains
Some people have all the luck and don't appreciate it
while others just throw it away

Not me. I work day and night just to pass and stay on the team
"Get it done" is my motto
When a test or paper is coming up, forget the parties
I know life is not fair, but how about a bit of balance?

Access my resources is the key to success
A tutor, or tutors I should say
One for math, another for English, and my folks help
If I fall through the cracks, it won't be for a lack of effort

Chance Hall

We all laugh as Mom and Dad
share high school memories
Mom skipped class - plenty
Just said she was a TA
Dad giggles when he tells about the
deer head in the girls' bathroom

But then they look disappointed when
the teacher says I left the locker room early
For crying out loud, who cares
Two minutes early! Oh my, a major crime!
They shake their heads and say,
"He's like that at home."

I just think, "A chip off the old block."
The PE teacher even took the time
to call home when I hit Boone's little brother
He of all people should know it's not easy
to stop when playing full court basketball
It was only a bloody lip. Cry baby!

Then the fat, old geezer told me to do push-ups
Yeah, I don't think so
Even got mad when I flipped a towel at David
like all the guys don't mess around in the locker room
He got mad when I tackled Robert at lunch
First, he wants me to be active and then not so much

Now, the VP wants me to serve Saturday school
Says I was egging on a fight
I was just running with the crowd after
Zach told us there was a fight under the flagpole
Ramsey said I threatened to beat him up
I didn't but I probably will now. Pansy

So, it's no big deal, I didn't do it,
accidents happen, everyone was doing it
No way am I going to check in daily
before and after school

Ramsey Stuart

Bros before hoes
That doesn't mean we aren't interested
We just know how to prioritize
but Bree definitely has my attention

Each whirl, twirl and spin provokes me
We could practice some moves
stretch a little – be flexible
work up a sweat and get acquainted

All the cheerleader chicks
know more than they let on
Their moves get us all riled up
In fact, Buck and I struggled after halftime

Probably why we thrashed the locker room
had to expel some energy somehow
Imagine what we would have done if we'd lost
but that team offered no challenge

Well, the school suspension wasn't all bad
It created space between me and
that psycho Edwards girl
She actually thought we'd date – in public

Yeah, well
always keep 'em guessing
Football, friends, females, and fun
What else is needed?

Jolene Edwards

I may never be able to trust a boy again
Maybe nobody! Never in my whole life
Jolene Stuart sounded good
I practiced writing it. Then,
Ramsey left a scar on my heart

We were each other's lab partners
When my sleeve touched the Bunsen burner
Ramsey crushed the flames while
igniting my desire. He saved my life

His smile was sincere; I could tell he cared
He walked me to my next class
even though he said it was on his way
My heart stopped, literally stopped

He asked me out on a date
Excited, I quickly shouted, "Yes"
When I suggested a place, he laughed
"Just joking," and walked away

The next day we had another science lab
I was hoping for another spark
I flirted and asked about our weekend plans
He stared mouth open, "You're not my type"

I put my head down and cried
Tears flowed uncontrollably
They were like a waterfall of misery
The teacher let me go to the bathroom
When I got back, Ramsey had moved seats

Holly Cooper

I pretty much just want to end life
But honestly! It's not like I would ever hurt myself

The school counselor tells me to look at the evidence
She says there are signs of distress

I shrug, "If your mom died, when you were ten,
you would be distressed too"

Yes, I have low grades, but I'm not stupid
I'm just not interested; they call it unmotivated

Ms. Hawks calls it underachieving; wants me in a group
Thinks talking to others will ease my frustration

My math teacher won't give me another book
Like it's my fault the other one turned up missing

I want a driver's license, which means I need to pass
but dangling that carrot isn't going to change things

I suppose saying that I was raped is attention seeking
Next time I'll say nothing. It really doesn't matter

The school resource officer said there is no evidence
It's a he said – she said situation

Ms. Hawks asked me to number my level of concern
She gave me a 10; I said 2 – Why worry?

So much unnecessary fuss

Lewis Livermore

I've been collecting paperwork all year long
You name it; I've got it
Enough to wallpaper my room
tardies
Saturday school
referral slips
calls to office
bullying citations
suspensions
detentions
smoking tickets

I get why I should come to school
even understand why being on time is important
but a ticket for bullying?
They've got to be kidding

When the principal told me to apologize
I did
What the hell does he mean
my apology was not sincere?

How else can I say I'm sorry?
and when it happened, I said,
"No hard feelings."

Stuart was right there beside me
He said he didn't hear nothin' wrong
Then they suspended me from a game
'spose it gives me some street cred

The team lost by 2 TD
Sure, wasn't my fault
They only hurt the team and our record
Thought I was being taught a lesson
Instead,
they learned a lesson

Ryan Wardle

People always say tell someone. Let others help you
So, I did. I stayed after class and bared my soul
I let Ms. K. know I had no lunch money
She gave me some graham crackers. That was nice

Once, just once, I went to the counselor – never again
When she heard there was nobody at my house,
she called home. Mom answered the phone even though
she doesn't respond to my calls

When I told the V.P. Tom Marston was bullying me
He talked to Tom who, of course, denied it
The V.P. made me stand in front of Tom and identify him
It was like poking a bear with a stick

In my English paper, I wrote about living alone
The teacher graded it with red marks but didn't say anything
What did I think she was going to do? Take me home with her?
Mom does have the house as her mailing address

Others gather during lunch at tables in the cafeteria
As they eat, they share food with friends and laugh
I don't have any food to share and
they would prob'ly laugh at me, not with me

Tom Marston

I signed my name to the citation
Not a ticket
A simple fine of $50.00
Bully

Ryan deserved to be called names
Little wannabe
He earned the name
Punk

The school cop wore a badge
Fake authority
Man, give it a rest
Pig

I sneered and spit with scorn
I accepted the paper and tore it up
without hesitation
Jerks

No skin off my nose
Just wait until I get Ryan alone
I'll show him
Narc

Kellen Labate

Coach says the definition of character is
When you act the same way when someone is watching or not
I told him that's me. I don't try to impress
He said, "That's not what I mean."

Huh.

Chance says I missed the point but couldn't explain it
He's kind of a pleaser, says he wants to be respected
I say respect isn't earned like that
A guy must stand up for himself

Now, the real kiss-up is that ginger,
David Clark, a major brown-noser
really pushes my buttons
so, I push back - a little

He tries to ignore me, takes whatever I dish out
needs to grow some balls
See, I treat him the same whether
someone is watching or not

Douglas Nash

The new Underarmor Cam Highlight
football cleats are wicked
I will be runnin' in style
When I kick ass this season,
only the best will do

The newly designed Xenith helmets are out
I'm not wearing the team headgear
that's like sharing a jockstrap
Gettin' my own
It's happening!

Better to be prepared with proper protection
After four concussions,
it's better to be safe than sorry
but I must grab this opportunity
No pain; no gain

Next year I will stand out to the recruiters
I must look good from top to bottom
Coach will make me team captain
Ah - and the scouts,
they will notice me

Nobody will tell me I can't play
The game must go on, and I am the game
Mom, my old man, and the coach
can shelf their concussion concerns
Relax!

Daniel Outland

I scan the defense to read the plays
I observe others to identify what's trending
When girls flirt, I understand their signals
but words I can't read
Sports drive me to work hard
If working hard would help the letters make sense
I would be a 4.0 student
Instead, my grades are the result of my charm
and a lot of help from friends

Bethany Crumbs

My wheelchair creates acceptance
My handicap suggests
I am special
within a school where
being the same is the goal
I am small, loved
The school mascot

Kids love to push my chair
and to be seen with me is like
a badge of honor
to rise to a higher
level of heaven
They are generous
Accepting

Any day I would prefer
to be normal
to be ignored or left alone
I would rather be bullied
because I am fat, ugly,
awkward,
or smell bad

Just not patronized
I am Bethany

Anna Carver

His little sister
Someone's lab partner
The girl in the third row
The body in seat 16
The one eating alone
The blonde everybody knows

In science, I'm Abby
English, they call me Ann
But Anna – never. I answer
My writing isn't distinguishable
If I forget to put my name on a paper
I'm a 0 in the gradebook

I smile; I laugh; I talk
but I never ask questions
I color in the lines and fill in the blanks.
My GPA is 3.0 mostly, sometimes 3.5
I dress in fashion and wear a stylish haircut
I go unnoticed

Levi Klipp

Yeah, sure,
school's important
That doesn't mean it should control my life
Graduation?

Oh, Yeah
I'll petition
Pro'bly won't graduate 'til next year
since they stole my credits

Only 34
Yeah, 34 absences this year
Like it is necessary to sit in class everyday
Can you believe they want me to retake english?

This school sucks!
I know how to read
They have to give me an education
It's the law

I am entitled to a diploma
It's important to my future
It's not the journey but the destination
I will walk because I earned it

Luis Guzman

Damn that Levi
He be messin' with his future
So much for a best friend
if he don't get
his butt back to school

Oh man,
Ava is nothing but trouble
I'm gonna make that girl stop hanging
with those cabronas
Leila's bad, and Ava knows it

Now Sue
She is fire I want to touch
Even if I get burned
Maybe Friday night
we could build a bonfire – make it HOT

Sue Udell

Mom works all night and doesn't come home
I hate the quiet of an empty house
Yet, I slept in . . . again

A reused dress, flip-flops and no makeup
I simply avoid mirrors
Out of sight, out of mind

For all they know, I plan this look
Never let them see me sweat
Cool, Classy, Calm

"It is what it is."
That's my motto for survival
When people look at me, they see a survivor

I survive being alone
Survive cooking my own meals
Survive living in a dirty house
Survive neglect
Yes, I survive
Will I ever thrive?

Leila Kovecev

There are worse things I could do
It's not like I robbed a bank!
So, I like to have fun

Boys say they enjoy my company
I know I enjoy theirs

But girls stab me in the back
So dramatic
They say nice things to my face
They ask for the Saturday night details

Then gossip:
    "She let him . . ."
    "She used his . . ."
    "They ended up . . ."

Well, yeah! That's what boys and girls do
It's not like I promise but don't deliver
What's their problem?

I hear Luis is going to the bonfire
I 'spose hanging with Ava ain't the worst
There is a benefit, her brother

Luis, never lets her out of sight
So, where she goes I go
Let's do this

Ava Guzman

Luis thinks I'm stupid
I know how to manage in his world
I know Ma only sees what she's shown
I know Papa works to pay the bills and plays to his pleasures
I know to not trust Leila

But I also know my way out
Education

I will be a doctor even though
    Luis thinks I am stupid
    Ma can't see the future
    Dad is stuck in the moment
    and Leila wants to tease life

I can have fun now
and find my future
Sure, sometimes I wonder. . .
College is my goal
Luis isn't hurting anything by standing guard

Noel Mathison

The science teacher talks about photosynthesis
oxygen, sun, water, trees, leaves
I stare out the window
watch a squirrel dodge a car

The coach's whistle pulls my attention
I continue the circle track toward him
always returning to where I start
The air on the field is freshly suppressive

The English teacher points out the novel's symbols
the tree, knothole, branches, the paper
glides across my desk
swept by the breeze from the window

Papers rustle, books close, and voices erupt
The teacher's voice is swallowed
by the movements and the bell
The metal chair legs scratch the linoleum

I am pushed through the door to the hall
like a salmon returning to spawn
Swimming within a school of cool indifference
knowing as I follow my instincts, I slowly die

Sherri Wine

Puppies! Our basset hound has fourteen!
Mom and Dad were going to have her spayed
Instead, they gave into my pleading
One – just ONE litter
Who knew Nanna would have FOURTEEN puppies

It's up to me to care for them
Keep them clean and fed
They can really make trouble
Spreading food, spilling water, and pooping
I can keep one if I raise my grades

Each puppy has a distinct personality:
Jim and Pam are inseparable
Stanley always lays in the back corner; he's fat
The one climbing on top of the others is Angela
When I feed them, Kevin is the first to eat
Dwight's kind of a dog snob
Phyllis makes a little, high pitched whine
Meredith sleeps on her back and wants her belly rubbed
Kelly's yelps call for attention; she's kind of demanding
Mom thought Oscar was a girl at first, turns out he's a boy
Andy constantly whimpers softly, like he is singing
The clumsy one who trips over his own feet is Michael Scott
The biggest one is Daryl, twice the size of the others
Toby is the runt that the others pick on
I sit and watch them for hours

Sally Quann

We planned so many adventures for the summer
swimming,
shopping,
gossiping
during the day

Sleeping on the tramp,
eating popcorn,
watching movies
at night

Sage, Sherri, and Sally
The three silly salamanders
celebrating summer

Then those puppies were born
Now that's all anyone talks about
Sure, they're cute
but kind of smelly
a lot of work
They make my skin itch
and my eyes water

Sherri's house is the place to hang
or was
Now, it's a place to avoid unless I want
bulging eyes like a troll,
to weep like a widow and
to breathe like a pug on a hot day

Sage Oland

My mom won't allow a pet in the house
No animals!
That's a refrain embedded in my mind
Pictures of horses, dogs, and even pygmy goats
cover the walls of my bedroom and locker

Some girls want a boyfriend
maybe someday
I simply want a pet
Everyday this summer, I'll be at Sherri's house
pettin', cuddlin', and lovin' those pups

It's nobody's business why I can't have a pet
Sherri asked once,
"Why are your folks so set against animals?
They are so strict."
"Yeah, it's not fair," I agreed

Not fair that my brother teases and hurts animals
Killed my cat
They say he has violent tendencies
but Sherri has puppies and I
can't wait to play with them

Wolf Trovato

We sat in the damn meeting for two hours
They asked questions and answered all
themselves
Called it a safety inventory
I'm not even sure why I had to be there

My old man showed up late
but at least he showed up this time
Looking his best in grease-stained coveralls
with grease under his fingernails
What did they expect?

Does he talk about hurting himself?
    Check

Has he ever mentioned suicide?
    Check
They talk like I am not in the room

Are there weapons in the home?
    Check

Are they inaccessible – out of reach or locked?
    Check

Has he ever brought a weapon to school?
    Keys with one filed to a sharp point
    He has an affinity to sharp objects
    He likes to cut things up

Can you give an example?
    Clothing, coats, blankets, sheets

What do the keys unlock?
    Front door, shed. . . gun safe

Do you feel threatened at home?
    No. But we had to call the cops last week

They did ask me one question
Who is your hero?
    Hitler

Why?
    He was a smart man.

Does this team feel Wolf is a safety threat?
    Check

To himself or others?
All the above

Mickey Slotham

A warrior of notoriety, to be battled,
bowed to, and conquered
Equipped with weapons:
swords, artillery, rapiers, and bludgeons
I lead because they follow

In this world, I am
more than a student, son, or brother
I create my world by leveling up
purchasing the weapons of protection
and using isolation to conceal my mortality

Each friend and foe has an identity
We never meet face to face
At least not in our mortal form
because in the screen, we are immortal

My anonymity provides my armor
So that when defeated or disgraced
I can remain a strong, proud opponent
by reinventing myself and building a new identity

People, who think they know me, call me Mickey
It is in this world of flesh and blood,
lacking anonymity, that I feel pain through
the stab of words, stares and accusing looks

Beyond the screen is my existence
I am Mardig, a world warrior

Laura Smits

Amazing Grace how sweet the sound
That saved a wretch like me
Dad's in jail; Mom's in the ground
Now, they will let me be

I once was lost but now I'm found
Was blind but now I see
My body lacks a heart that pounds
My lungs can finally breathe

T'was fear that caused my heart to break
And fears are now no more
I search for ways to heal the ache
Gone's all feeling at my core

Now, I'm a leaf without a stem
To attach me to a tree
A barren branch; unfruitful limbs
I look up from on my knees

Standing open is a door
A call to walk on through
A brand-new day, a chance to soar
As fresh as the morning dew

Christie Ehlers

It will be nice to get away from these halls
eyes watch
mouths label:
Jocks, Goths, Intellects, Slackers, Players
Geeks, Gays, Hipsters, Preps, Gamers

It doesn't matter to me what color people are
What they do or
Who they do it with

Grams says,
"Hearts like doors open with ease
When you say thank you
and if you say please."

She also taught me it's best to forgive,
    "Do unto others as you
    would want them
    to do unto you."

Grams is smart
for someone who never attended
school past fifth grade,
    "A smile is the one thing that multiplies
    when you give it away."

So, I compliment other students
    Thank teachers
        Show kindness
            Forgive
And smile

Ken Lee

He says to call him Dad
Like hell I will
A dad is supposed to care about their kid
John doesn't care about me
I don't give a damn about him

Apparently, Mom cares about him
I sure don't know why
After beating her almost daily,
she supports his behavior
Even testified on his behalf in court

The old man is getting what he deserves
Mom is waiting to welcome him home
Not me
I am outta here
Gone

Kendall says I can crash at her house
Graviet's place is an option
I want to see Dad - my real dad
I haven't seen him in ten years, but he never hit me
Maybe he has an extra bed

Johnny Graviet

I made bad choices
Absences piled up - grades tanked
Support from encouraging
friends helped

But not until I realized my pain
did I start to trust
my parents
realizing they are on my side

Lynn helped me see

The note was not intended for me
but I read it
I rescued her from humiliation
She saved my life

It started out simple
She organized my notebook
Neither of us realized she was
shaping my future

That's when my grades improved
School became tolerable
Her friends welcomed me
while I unintentionally connected

Now my folks smile when I get home
and I go home
They even let Ken move in for awhile
at least until things settle down at his house

When I look at Ken,
I see what life used to be
When I look at Lynn,
I see what life might be

Lynn Day

I was passing a note
to Katie
It made it halfway
down the row
Johnny Graviet
to my dismay
interrupted the route
He opened it
He read it
He smiled
I wanted to die

Johnny
intercepted
my secrets

When the bell rang,
we walked
into the hall
I wanted to run
but Johnny stood
between me
and my next class
blocking my escape
He lightly kissed me
on the cheek,
then walked away

His shoes were black
His pants were a little short
Diamonds painted his socks

Without looking up
I went to my next class
wondering why

Kendall Young

I figure I'm lucky
Dad doesn't hit me
Mom can't be bothered with me
unless she needs something
out of reach of the couch

I am better off than Ken
I have a safe home to go to
I get a good night sleep
I have my own bedroom
My folks don't mind having me around

Besides, there is usually food in the fridge
especially on the first of each month
right after the check comes
Someone always cleans about that time
for the monthly welfare inspection

The police know Ken's address by heart
He knows them by their first name
According to him, it's always the same
His stepdad, John, starts drinking
He's a mean drunk

His mom gets mouthy about John not working
He tells her to shut-up; she doesn't
So, he backhands her to speed up the process
The neighbors call the cops
Starsky and Hutch show up to stop the disturbance

Life's not so bad from my angle
There are few restrictions at home
School provides a free lunch and a place to chill
I have a solid reputation
If I go with the flow, everything's just great

It all works for me
Like I said before, I got a room over my head
I have my health, food, and the tv works
What more can a gal ask for?
Hugs are overrated

Carolyn Barnett

I am so excited for a break
Olive and I have a plan for each day
starting with a long walk along the canal
to celebrate the beginning of summer

I hope those ducklings still have their fuzz
Olive has wanted to see them for days
Since her mom got sick, there isn't much free time
She's expected to help mom

I want to tell her how the baby ducks
follow their mama in a straight line
most the time
and how Mama squawks when one wonders off

It's always Domino
who gets separated
He seems to get distracted
Stops to examine things
a rock
flowers
bugs
even his own feet
Then he ventures off
on a different path

Domino is so cute when he chases dandelion fluff
What would he do if he caught it?
I am going to tell Olive all the things
I can't say at school for fear of hearing

"Thupid Carolyn thulks funny"
Why can't they see beyond this lisp?

Olive Norton

The summer break is going to be sooo long
With mom sick, we must be quite
It's best to not even turn on the radio
I kinda dread it; I get lonely

Carolyn keeps talking about hanging out
How can I tell her I can't leave Momma?
When I am at school, a caretaker comes
During summer, the job is mine

I love Mom! I will do anything for her
It just makes the days long
I clean quietly
Read a book silently
Daydream in my head
Sometimes my own voice
makes me jump
Lord knows money is tight
This is my way to help

The school library opens once a week
Auntie says she'll sit with mom
so I can check out new books,
my source of friends and adventures

In the spring, Dad says I get new clothes
Maybe the name calling might stop
at least slow down
Thrift store whore is an ugly phrase

I don't want to get my hopes up
because family comes first
But I think and fantasize about
the possibilities a lot

Zach Turner

Kids laugh when I am in the room
They think I am funny
I am
Teachers, not so much

Mrs. Ober says I cause distractions
Is it my fault that everyone looks at me?
She makes me work in the hall
Hall's fine with me

I can't be in a classroom with a substitute
What do they think I will do? Eat them?
I sit and mind my own business
What?
I just meet their expectations

Carolyn cries, "Teacher!" when my feet touch her chair
"Thop that! It wath not an acthident!"
How can I not laugh at that? It was an accident
My chair backed into retainer girl

That pencil slipped between my fingers;
It's not my fault that it hit Robert's face
Chance understands 'cuz he gets singled out too
The teacher calls him out for things he didn't do

My grades are all passing, and my work's turned in
Why make such a big deal about guys' games?
The girls giggle - even when they complain
I don't get what the big deal is

Eve McClair

Mom stood beside me
The pit in my stomach grew
The line snaked through the cafeteria
with hardly any familiar faces
It trailed through the doors
out to the parking lot
I figured it would be a year
much like the others

With a name that starts with M
I would be in the middle
A good chance I would sit
beside Noel Mathison and Brady Mead
My sisters told me what to expect, but I
never expected Gabriela Blair to
cut in line like we were best friends
We hugged and talked about the summer

Mom raised her eyes then shrugged
No one mentioned her cutting
Then Gabby asked, "Do you want
to try out for cheerleader?"
"No way," was my response
I almost looked to see who she was asking
"I could do that. I have nothing to lose."
was my thought

I wore that cheerleading uniform
three times a week
Now, I will do anything for Gabby
She changed my life
Next year at registration,
I won't be standing
in line with my mother

That's so way not cool

Gabriela Blair

I have two friends,
Eve and Brooke
I feel sorry for both

Thanks to me Eve's not a wallflower
Should have seen her at registration
with her mom!

Brooke, on the other hand,
won't be seen with her mother on a bet
She could benefit from a little supervision

As my friends,
they are now somebody
Somebodies others want around

Eve is now on the cheerleading squad
She stands beside me in the front row
Thinks I am a god – or goddess
But then I guess I am
Who else could have opened the door
to the most popular group at school
With my help, she is dazzling

Brooke was harder to reinvent
Not easy, like getting a nobody seen
She was noticed for the wrong reasons
First goal, garbage those short shorts
Is she oblivious? "Party Girl" on her butt?
It reads as an advertisement
Way too direct, girls must be more subtle

When we walk down the hall, heads turn
We look good, not slutty, but glam
Even Jade is envious

Queen Bee Wannabee?
Not me
Queen Gabby

Brooke Lyons

Gabby is a lifesaver
For reals!
She changed my life
mostly for the better

I kinda miss Brittany
We've been friends forever
Sometimes sacrifices must be made
Mom even agrees
I notice Brit eats lunch alone
When I ask Gabby if she can sit with us
She laughs
I don't know what is funny

Dad was fuming about
sexual harassment
He even complained to the principal
when Bodi slapped my butt,
He went through the roof
Don't want to know what Dad would do
If he knew Bodi asked,
"How much do you make on the street?"

Jesse once called me a tramp
Now he actually eats at our table
That shows you Gabby's power
A lifesaver I say

Bodi Harrington

In my opinion, Brooke asked for it
A little slap on the butt never hurt
Most girls like it; they giggle
I mean she was wearing a butt billboard
I see why they're called hot pants

I respect girls; only give compliments:
dabomb, swagalicious, hot chick
I don't insult them like Zach
He told Dora her face is good birth control
I would never insult a girl like that

The other guys understand
It's locker room talk:
"Give me some of that"
"She said no but meant yes"
There is a lot of testosterone floating around

Guys have to assert their masculinity
Pro'bly why when they run around in their boxers
they slap each other on the butt
Or why when they walk 'round naked with other guys
They like to brag a little – exaggerate a lot

> "I had to show her how, but it was good"
> "She has what we call an oral fixation"
> "She was easy. But so was her sister"

At the party everyone was looking at Colleen's pic
Why'd she send it if she didn't want us looking?
No different than surfing the internet now-a-days
Every girl at that party was a tease
Naw, there is no way Jade was a virgin
Get real!

Jade Baker

I don't remember much
It was supposed to be a party
You know
like were people have fun
Celebrating the end of the year
Pre-graduation

We drank a little
Maybe a little more than planned
But I never planned what happened
Nobody plans to get
Raped

I don't remember much
After I woke up
except the pain
The lack of emotion
I cried when they told me
I was found alone
Unclothed
Bruised
Exposed

The morning after,
friends texted
Said they wanted to check how I was
Someone sent flowers
Seems appropriate because
part of me died

Days after, everyone acted like
it didn't happen
but it did

My world changed

A week from now
I will walk across the stage
Someone will hand me
a diploma
Everyone says it will be
a new beginning
I keep thinking
this is the end

Sparrow Gilmore

I try not to do things alone,
not even wash the dishes
Solitude causes me to get lost
in the dark thoughts of my head

The shrink says I have anxiety
and suffer from depression
My brain chants I am inadequate
convincing me of my worthlessness

When surrounded by people
their dramas demand attention
silencing the mantras that sanction
my insignificance, irrelevance, ineptness

I just can't control what happens
I have nothing to contribute
When I was in the hospital, it was better
They told me what to do and when to do it

Every day is a struggle
The simpler the task the harder
Complex tasks silence the refrains
Difficulty is essential

The bothersome part of it all
is there is not one big thing
that made me this way
Nothing I can pinpoint

Life's provided a loving family
Since I've come home,
I am trying to find my zone
my sense of balance

When I try to run away
a shadow follows a body
So, headphones plug my ears
and music sweeps me away

Jenna Arnold

When I am with Bree,
I've learned to look confused

I know to dress like Sparrow
short skirts and crop tops

I watch. Peyton gets happy
when she's the center of attention

I listen to whoever stands next to me
I nod
I stand in the middle of the group
unnoticed
My friends define me
creating my identity

Jesse's attendance at my party
will cement my reputation
My bikini will assure
I'll be remembered
Everyone will know
I am somebody

Unlike Dora Quick,
I am not a social fruit fly
By being with them,
I am one of them

Jesse Vaughn

Whoever designed tight pants wasn't a teenage boy
No wonder my grades are low
with all the female distractions
some days studying is far from my mind

Damn! I walk by Jade's desk ten times to sharpen my pencil
Her aqua top catches my attention
I am captivated - not by the shirt
and not by old Mrs. Greyford's math lesson

Jenna walks away after inviting me to her swim party
I just stare at every wiggle, jiggle, and shake
If she looks as good in a swimsuit, Shit!
I won't be able to get out of the water

Sparrow sure takes her time digging through her locker
It is directly above mine
Her short skirts from my angle make coming
to school both a blessing and a curse

I walk around with a notebook strategically in front of me
Damn my uncontrollable body
Girls in tight pants, low shirts, and short skirts
make every day at school a hard place to be

Girls are a great attendance incentive for high school guys
I'm just saying, it's a tough life
but a free and public education is mandatory for all
A guys gotta do what a guy's gotta do

Bree Harvey

Yeah, I know what they say about me
It's just when I stress
I get inside my head and can't get out
Confusion makes me look like
the dumb blonde they think I am

I am going to fail
I just know it
No matter how hard I try
bad grades pop up on my phone
Every time a teacher updates grades

Teachers aren't very good
I should have an A
Mom got me a tutor
who tries to help me understand
When she has the pencil, it makes sense
When I work on the packet,
a hurricane swirls in my head

The more I stress,
the more I confuse myself
When I can't calm down,
the anxiety gets worse

Slow down
Deep breath
Relax

Peyton Birch

How does she always know?
I can text without even looking
at it under my desk
What's the big deal anyway?

She has to raise my grade
I emailed her after the final
Dropped me from 89% to 88%
It only seems fair to round it up

Every teacher rounds 89% to an A
88% is only one point more
so it shouldn't be a big deal
I really need an A

Jenna is good to have as a friend
but not necessarily a good friend
Passing me that cheating chain
helped me learn the information

Bree is not as dumb as she acts
Such an attention whore
I should tell the teacher that she's the one
who started texting copies of the test

Then maybe she'd understand
it's not my fault
I never asked for the answers
They just appeared

Dora Quick

A pool party! It sounds so exciting
I'll have to ask Jenna when it is
She goes out of her way
to make me feel included
when I follow her around

The gossip flows like a waterfall
At school everyone talks
I know I can't believe everything
but there must be some truth
otherwise, why would they say so

For instance, I don't believe Peyton
She said Jenna insulted me
  We are good friends
Then she called Eve a social chameleon
Eve seemed upset; then she laughed
Wonder why she was crying later at lunch

Zach's comment about me hurt
But when he winked at me
I knew he didn't mean it
He is always cracking jokes
Everyone expects him to be funny

  People are whispering about Jade
  Something happened at the party
  but nobody will say what
  It can't be that big of a deal or
  Jade would say something

Well, rumors are just part of high school
Someone said the cops came to the last party
I heard it was so loud the neighbors called them
Bodi treats girls bad but nobody cares
It's just who he is

Liam Endicott

I am so sick of hearing,
"Take your hat off"
What is their problem?
Don't they have anything better to do?
like teach?

Besides, we were just doing the schoolwork
the shop teacher taught us
So, we checked to see if it worked
It was so worth the trouble
We'll always be remembered

All it took was a nine-volt battery
some steel wool,
PRESTO –
Boy, did it work!
A fire started
in the boys' locker room
No big deal
until the alarm went off

It was LOUD
The big guy was mad
Interrupted finals
The students were thankful
gave everyone a break
evacuated the building
Fresh air was appreciated

Totally bodacious!

Candis Clair

My parents are so embarrassing!
I can't believe I have any friends at all
let alone a boyfriend
I need to hear that again
I – have - a - boyfriend

Before Mom met him,
I didn't know what to expect
She thinks she's funny – she's not
She asked Brian, "So you're the flavor of the week?"
He smirked, "Yeah, chocolate."

Well, that cut the tension
They both laughed and seemed to hit it off
Guess that means summer will have
hot days and hot nights
'Cuz, I HAVE A BOYFRIEND

Shawn's dad is livid that we are dating
Not that it's any of his business
I don't care what his dad says about mixed race
relationships. We are awesome together
He must let it go. We're just kids

But then, Shawn isn't so happy either
He actually said I'm not right for Brian
It's not like we're getting married,
having babies, starting a family
Their beliefs are so yesterday!

Shawn Bishop

Everyone is prejudiced
It means to pre-judge
I do; who doesn't
    Old people are expected to drive slowly
    Teenagers swear
    Moms cook and clean
    Dads bring home the money

Sure, I know this isn't always the case
They are preconceived notions
So why buck the system?
Why set yourself up for trouble?

No way am I a racist
Brian Thatcher is one of my best buds
but why does he have to date
a white girl? He's black

Candis and I have been friends since preschool
I've watched her grow up and know
she understands this is not right
Interracial relationships are wrong

Mom and Dad agree
We need to stay with our own kind
The next thing you know they will ask
for our approval

Naw – that ain't gonna happen
We can all be friends and hangout
but dating is where I draw the line
We need to set some standards

Brian Thatcher

When I came to this community,
I wondered if I would ever fit in
Everyone was welcoming
They accepted me
        on the football field
        in the classroom
        even at church

Sometimes all the guys and I would
stay up all night playing video games
eating pizza and drinking cola
I felt like one of the group

When I started dating Candis
things changed without any
identifiable differences
I was still on the team with the guys

I couldn't put my finger on it until
Mr. Taupe, the math teacher, asked
if I thought it was a good idea
to date "That Candis girl"

I shrugged thinking, "Why not?"

Man, did I figure out why not!
People I thought were my friends
saw our color differences as a barrier
like oil and vinegar, they don't mix

I stopped seeing color. Thought they had too
until people stopped making eye contact
Started making subtle comments
It wasn't what they said but what they didn't

Shawn clearly stated the problem, his problem
He asked, "Why date a girl who's out of reach?"
It dawned on me I could look but not touch
I could be involved never embraced

Nick Eldridge

As an observant watcher,
I am excluded
and seclude myself
Boys walk the halls in packs
Acknowledge each other with nods
I follow a few paces behind

During lunch, I never eat
Instead, move slowly to merge
Seemingly a member of many groups
In the bathroom,
the walls hold my attention
No eyes reflect in the mirror

No footprints remain where I walk
The absence of my picture in the yearbook
goes unnoticed
like my absence of emotion
By being alone without attachments
I am one with many

Jack Pitman

I like the challenges of life
Schoolwork not being a challenge

I observe the world around me - my domain
Watch for opportunities
to elevate my status among those
who think they are important:
Athletes, cheerleaders, Christians, Boy Scouts
They all follow the rules
granting others power

I always look adults in the eyes
Not because I fear them but to show that I don't
My stares create suspicion
I know
Never turn my back to them
They never turn their backs on me
I talk little in a world that worships words

I may look ragged, however be wary
Looks are deceiving
With multiple watches on my right arm, I inspire
questions. But the answers are lies
The need to ask questions shows weakness
Time is controlled by
people who see relevance in the present

Body language is my mode of communication
My head nod offers acknowledgement
My handshake suggests promises
My words never incriminate
If I stay in your presence, it means interest
but don't be confused, I don't care
I withdrawal from a world that covets acceptance

In my world, the challenge is
the chance to make a deal to my benefit

Cliff Van Wagner

Team photos
Championship trophies
Broken records

We attended senior prom
Our tuxes displayed the school colors
even dyed my hair blue

My locker was on the top,
seniors over the juniors
I was king of the hill

We dominated at the pep rallies
controlled the hallways
ruled the school

The band trip to Cali was a highlight
The gang sat in the back of the bus
Made the underclassmen move

Graduation pictures
Announcements and diplomas
They will all walk

Kaleb Acuff's going to college
Guzman's gettin' a job with his dad
Harrison and Ben are going on a road trip

I will attend summer school
to earn a couple of failed credits
Then return to high school to earn the rest

I wonder if I'll be on a team next year
Go to the prom, travel to Cali – again
If so, with who?

From the bleachers, I will watch
the others walk - if I even go
School sucks crap!

Kaleb Acuff

Josh says my thinking is wishful
Yeah, I know the stats
Only 5% of high school students
get a full ride
Scholarships are few and far between
Only 10% of college students
who play get drafted

But I know what I can do
Best defensive player on the squad
Power hitter who gets on base
Great fielder with control
Superior speed
Awesome arm
Long range

I may not be the next Cal Ripken Jr.
He was and always will be the best
I may not steal bases like Ty Cobb
but I consistently cover the bases

The team knows I make the plays
Scouts watching the next game
will see me work my magic
On the field, the stats won't matter

Who says
I can't be
one of the
5 percent?

Josh Ingraham

If the teacher is going to drone on,
why can't I put my head on the desk?
I get so bored
I am barely able to stay awake

But knowing I have basketball,
a light shines at the end of the tunnel
I can make it
through each period of each day

Yet, the coach calls me in to say
He is benching me
Low grades
They can do that?

I don't dribble the ball in the classroom
Why do my grades matter on the court?
Makes no sense
They are two separate things

I move to the front, lift my head
The teacher continues to drone on
I work harder
My grade should be improving

The guys help get the work done
Kaleb quizzes me for tests
Real teamwork
John thinks I'm wasting potential

Entering the testing room is draining
Worse than starting a championship game
Mega stress
The waiting is traumatic

Again, the coach calls my name
This didn't turn out well last time
Grade check
The next game, I start!

Manuel Ibarra

We were undefeated
until the last game of the season
The team knew I was capable
They trusted me; I let them down
Rain pounded like a hammer
It matched my heartbeat
A rhythm established
We devised a plan to
guarantee victory

If everyone executed their part,
success was achievable
The ball flew
I jumped,
caught the aerial,
landed vertical,
dodged the defender,
leaped forward,
missed the goal line by half a yard

Going into the playoff, I felt guilt
Self-imposed maybe
I had to regain their trust
To be put in position
To be given the ball
To gain the advantage
To win

Just as so many times before
It came down to the last play
Moving on a wet field
Beating rain matched my heartbeat
I was ready for the win
We expected to win
We did

Edwin Cortez

Yeah, I am excited for summer
Can't wait to wake up everyday
to my old man's criticism

He doesn't get why I spend
all my free time reading
alone in my bedroom

"When I was a kid"
Yeah, he walked up hill - both ways
To school it was five miles - both ways

He tells me to get my nose out of the book
Act like a man
Do something useful

Books take me away
Create a new reality
Provide an exit from here

His salty attitude won't
detour my goals
It reinforces my dedication

He makes me feel like shit
I am indebted to him
for he's my motivation
My inspiration

Thanks, Dad

Brittany Padilla

Mom don't want another note in the mail
and NO home visits with a police escort
Why'd that principal bring a cop?
So, I miss a few days of school
It's not like the teachers want me there
Just another paper to grade
I heard them say so

Most times, it's hard to sleep
I'm up at 4 a.m. watching Sponge Bob
Nobody in my house is awake at that time
When I fall back asleep,
the bus leaves without me
It's actually a relief to the other students
That bus is way overcrowded

Them at the door say I must go to school
asked if there is food in the house
That set Mom off. What she said then
is mild compared to what she said later
"Take a good look at her.
She's ain't missin' any meals
There is usually stuff in the fridge."

That principal said they can get me free lunch
Said I don't eat. How'd she know that?
"Hell no! We ain't no charity case
She is supposed to pack a lunch the night before
If she don't, then she don't eat
It won't teach her anything if I bring her lunch
Now, is that all you want?"

When the door shut, Mom gave me the snake eye
Pursed her lips, "That better not happen again.
Get your ass to school.
If I have to crawl out of bed again this early,
your ass is grass. Get to school."
"Yes, ma'am."
I grabbed my empty backpack and started walkin'

Adam Cycle

My old man acts
like I am the first kid to get a couple F's
I fill out a daily tracking form
He says it's because he cares about me
He doesn't. It's to create the illusion
that he's a loving father

Every day get paper
Every period complete paper
Every assignment turned in
Every teacher must sign
Every day, every child a success

When I get home each day
Dad says to just lay it on the table
The papers pile up
like shit in a farmyard
A waste of time, energy, and resources

I will succeed in spite of them
What they don't get is
I don't need a tracking form.
I need to care
I don't

Shianne Yeager

I may have called her ideas stupid - not her
Just 'cuz I say something
doesn't mean I mean it
Allison continually blows things
way out of proportion
I mean really?
Why would I call her worthless?
I value her as my ADOPTED sister

I told her sorry –
I am truly sorry
she got the idea that
I don't like her
She is out of control
No grasp on reality
Blames her problems on me
Ungrateful bitch

My family opens our house
gives her a bed to use
provides her food
Now we must deal with
all the neighbors' questions
Complete the state's paperwork
She never stops to think
How we feel
I mean - really?

Allison East

They say home is where the heart is - whatever
Having a heart implies the ability to love
I could learn to love if I lived in one place with one family
The adoption agency said, "We have a family for you."

A forever family loves unconditionally. Know what that isn't?
They don't pack all your belongings in plastic sacks,
drop them off at school and say, "We didn't think it would be
this hard. We've had enough. She's damaged goods." No shit!

What did they think they were bringing home? A puppy?
After three failed foster parent placements
A failed adoption just follows suit
I expect no less. Rejection always comes

What'd they expect when my "sister" is so nasty
Never accepted me and in fact, she wishes me dead
Said, "I am sorry if I ever gave you the idea I liked you"
Hate to break it to her, but I never had that idea

After two years of being called fake, worthless, stupid, bitch
I started the believe it. The emotional pain was
overwhelming. No surprise because
I am the outsider who entered their world

The sleeping pills were just too much for the family
Not enough for me because I still walk these halls
but plenty for them to call it quits. Kind of like
one of those oxymorons the teacher talks about

Kenman Rue

It was a daring move to write
a love letter to Leah,
but I knew before leaving
I had to profess my admiration

I was waiting for Leah to respond
but can't wait forever to decide

I'll decline the International Scholarship
My opportunity to return

One year in the US is enough
not like an exchange student
can be a permanent citizen
It's time to go home

Valeri Kaiser

This sucks big time
The last day of school
I'm stuck in detention
Mom said I could go to the class picnic
then forgot to sign the permission slip
I only wanted to help
Apparently, writing your mom's signature is
forgery

Now the celebration
begins without me
While Leah flirts and gets phone numbers,
I pick up garbage in the parking lot
This is the worst day of my life
Sucks
Totally unfair

Leah didn't back up my story
She knows Mom said it was ok
but she's mad because
I used her locker
I don't know why it's such a big deal
It's closer than going upstairs
Not my fault the coke bottle leaked

She said she wasn't mad
Just reprint the English paper
It was the letter that pissed her off
The ink on the lines bled together
making it illegible
The paper stuck to the bottom
peeled off in pieces

With it, evaporated the address
Dissolved their relationship
and ours
She couldn't write back, and he didn't

Leah Johnson

Sure, I can rally the squad
look animated
sound enthusiastic
be a team player

But I know cheerleading
is a show like these tiny colored
barrettes in my hair,
all show with no purpose
While thinking what a bore,
I move through the motions,
practicing the drills so we are in sync
One temporary movement

I want to be loved
The one chance I had
was the letter that showed up
in my locker

Somebody saw me as an individual
noticed me
"You are beautiful."
He wanted to meet
likes my hair, smile, clothes, voice
All I had to do was write back
if interested
I AM!

Before I could write back
Valeri broke into my locker,
spilled her soda
leaving a syrupy mess
on the locker floor

All the papers stuck together
The ink smeared
The romance faded with the words
My admirer will remain a mystery

Tyler Fagg

Everyone around here is excited
like vacation is something exciting
Oh goody. Three months of imprisonment
At least in jail, I would get halfway decent food

Everyone is getting yearbooks signed
It's all so dumb – Why would I want another book?
Who would sign it anyway?
They have nothing to say that I want to hear

This locker is empty just as it has been all year
Not too hard to clean out
Sports are my reasons for school anyways
but I didn't play - low grades

But at least at home this summer
the jokes will stop. "Hey Fagg, got a date for the dance?"
"What's his name?" Assholes think they're funny
No name calling at home; no name at all

Blair Swenson

Once they got to know me it wasn't so bad
In fact, they started to accept me after
I penned every competitor in my weight division
Guess I had to prove myself

At first, they nicknamed me Camel
because of the way my singlet fit
Made fun of my short hair
Great for the helmet but bad style

Mom said entice them with a smile
I chose to kick their asses

I know I will never be in their social group
I'll probably always be alone in the locker room
but after the last match, I got a fist bump from Peter
and Eli Hess slapped me on the back
It is wicked fun

Eli Hess

Some people think I have a temper problem
They'd be surprised to know I am hungry
That may be hard to believe
I have plenty of money and food
and no, I am not anorexic

I am a wrestler
To compete in my weight class
sometimes starving myself is necessary
Hunger makes me a cranky,
short tempered athlete

Breakfast is egg whites and water
Cheese sticks and half a sandwich for lunch
Dinner's tuna sandwich and more water

Then, sweat off the pounds
It's what I do for weeks on end

The worst was when Dad held me back
in the eighth grade
Said it would give me time to grow
since I was small for my age
Provide an edge over the competition

No, the worst was taking math class online
when the school had nothing else to offer
I'd already passed their highest course

Wrestling is more than a sport
It's a way of life
I would rather be dead but not if I'd miss
the sound of a smack down
smell of perspiration

When it is all over
I fill satisfaction; no longer cranky
I eat my body weight
I am a wrestler; it's what a wrestler does

Peter Wright

Sure, my size helps but
my control is what makes me
a winner
I don't live to wrestle
but I damn sure do enjoy it
I've gotta make it work for me
I will never understand
the guys who are slaves
to the sport

I wrestle but
a wrestler is not my identity
It's just something I do
Suppose that's why I am
not intimidated by Blair
She's a real competitor
Doesn't matter if she is a girl
It's what she brings to the mat
It all about knowing what you want

Manuel Rodriquez

Yes, Ma'am
Yes, Sir
Look down, show respect
America is my home

Mamma taught me to act like a visitor
if we want to stay in our home
We must be seen and not heard
even though I was born here

Mamma is a good woman
Cooks, cleans, works hard
Papa puts food on the table
working long hours each day

I keep my grades up.
stay out of trouble,
and fill Papa's shoes
when he's not around

I translate for Mamma
She speaks no English
Reads only Spanish,
her mother tongue

Papa knows a little English
Allows him to be
a supervisor of a crew
of Mexicans

Mamma and Papa came
to America for a better life
Taught me the value of hard work
We work hard

We are not afraid of hard work
We understand there is only
One thing to be noticed for
hard work

Mitch Phelps

I hope my stupid comment doesn't get
Manuel in trouble
He has enough problems without me
I was just admiring the pic
The teacher said it's disrespectful
to call his wife hot. Glad he
didn't hear what else I said
Why is it on his desk
if he doesn't want us to appreciate it?

Manuel smirked at my words
His mamma would box his ears
commenting on a woman's figure,
a married white woman,
not acceptable
But I figure, a man displays
a picture of his wife in a bikini
he must be looking for comments

Aaron Burton

In the third grade, my teacher lied to me,
said I would grow over the summer
Oh, I grew - one inch - but I still wasn't
close to anyone else's height

I am short
Short people don't make the basketball team
or play football
Sports aren't high on the list of options

It wasn't until my freshman year in H.S.
that I found my thing. I sing and dance
Opening a door to the here and now
as well as my future

The first play I was in was *Harry Potter*
Daniel Radcliffe is only 5' 5"
Sarina can't pass up my moves on stage
Two years later, she is mine

I remember the moment, outside
laying on the grass, looking at the clouds
watching the white puffs shift and form
into a pig, a horse, a dinosaur

We laughed. Then the clouds parted to expose the sun
The billows framed the sun with a heart
I squeezed her hand and said,
"You have cleared the fog in my heart to expose my love."

From that moment, she has been my leading lady
This fall we both head off to college
I have an acting scholarship, Sarina a music scholarship
at the same university!

Yeah, I did finally grow, this year
Senior year, I auditioned and landed
the lead role in our last school production – *The Beast*
You guessed it, Sarina was Belle, my Beauty

Sarina Finch

Aaron is corny, a hopeless romantic
but I love him
He first told me he loved me
when we were watching the clouds
Made a cliché comparison
I almost laughed out loud

We are planning to go to the same college
rent a small apartment together

I don't know what the future holds
Who can predict the future?
I committed when we made love
but let's take it slowly and
experience each day
See what happens

I never promised a lifetime together
We are only in act one

Carolyn Anderson

Momma told me the red mark on my face
is a symbol of God's love
I am special
All the kids at school say it's an ugly scar
They tease and instead of playing chase
They run the other way

Then Lane enrolled in our school
Girls swarmed him
They all wanted to be his friend,
or more
We first talked when he saw me
reading *The Princess Bride*

He walked up and said, "I love the classics.
Always been a favorite."
I smiled,
continued reading, assuming
he would walk away. He didn't
I could feel his presence

The next day he was carrying –
you'll never guess –
The Princess Bride
He said hi, sat down
We read, ate and he helped me off the grass
I heard, "You're really pretty."

I remember putting my hand to my face,
traced my birthmark
My cheek was wet
I whispered, "No I'm not"
Turned my head away from him
Behind me I heard, "As you wish"

Lane Iverson

It was the first day at a new school when I noticed Carolyn
I saw her from the back, almost six feet tall with long hair
I mean really long, blonde hair. She walked with confidence
She never made eye contact with others
She never raised her head. Yet her movements showed
ease and determination
It was probably her clothes. They were comfortable,
casual, inviting
Nothing like the other girls who try to show off,
draw attention to what doesn't matter

Then at lunch I was bombarded with attention
from everybody but her
Insincere smiles
Attention isn't always good

Questions take
give nothing in return
People want to hear
not interested in knowing

I watched her on the grass reading
from across the courtyard
When I asked a guy her name, his shoulder's shrugged
Everyone I asked didn't know
or said something different
So, I sat next to her
I was going to introduce myself
but the quiet was comfortable

The next day I ate lunch beside her
After eating, I opened *The Princess Bride*,
the book I noticed her reading the day before
She noticed, smiled,
continued reading
When I asked her if she wanted a friend,
She softly replied, "As you wish."

Lucy Reid

Yes, I know CPR
It's my one claim to fame
When that boy collapsed
in front of me,
I just moved on instinct
They say I saved his life

Cardiopulmonary
resuscitation is a
lifesaving procedure
that keeps the heart
beating
until a professional arrives

I simply do what's right
Nobody has to tell me
I don't need to hear
praise or thank you
The reward is knowing
I make a difference

Kayla Laird

A smile covers my feelings
Nothing seems to matter
Unmotivated
Unwanted
Unloved
Weights shackle
legs
arms
waist
Pull me down

With each day my smile grows
to camouflage emotions
afraid
ignored
confined
by the darkness
of a damp hole

Dazed to my core
ready to explode with
sadness
apathy
fizzling
like an open, shaken soda

Empty of contents
sinking beyond the
stickiness
hollowness
existence
exit by letting go

Evaporate

My smile fades
The façade crumbles
Silent words scream
I have a final plan

Tiffany Summers

People are important to me
I want to be a friend but
being present is tiring
Each text, each call
drained my strength

My life has few problems
but I sink from concerns
It isn't fair; I am so lucky
while others
in the same neighborhood
church, school,
with the same friends
endure daily despair

After days – no weeks
offering,
providing support,
someone made a new rule
I must find time for myself
be a kid

Following their rulebook
I turned off my phone

Her calls and texts
went unanswered
Now that she doesn't call,
I crave to hear her voice,
share her pain,
Be there for her

Grief doesn't define
my torment
I will never again
feel happiness
be a kid
She will never text again

Dallin Puegh

When we were little, kids thought it funny
They'd plug their noses
when I came in the room
I'd laugh but it wasn't amusing
Puegh they would sing

I hate that last name
I asked Dad if I could change it
He just laughed,
"What doesn't kill you makes
you stronger. I lived with it."

Well, I don't feel stronger
So, what's the other option?
I ignore, pull inside my shell
like a tortoise trying to hide
Really, I seek protection

When they asked why I did it
I shrugged my shoulders
    The dark space in the dryer
    looked so comforting
Then I fell asleep

The teacher yelled bloody murder
when she discovered my body,
but there was no physical death
just emotional

At least I don't cry at school
I've learned to control that
until I get home

Brady Mead

Nobody believes me
A simple cough can
send me to bed
for a week
The hospital is often
not far away

My immune system
can't battle germs
Kids at school think
it's cool to get
so many days off
They are wrong

I just want to be normal,
have some friends
I even get
excited about homework
I live in a
cocoon of solitude

Shirley Goodman

Mom placed an ad in the paper
For Sale: Horse
The first two days
I was glad
nobody called
I didn't want anyone to buy her

The third day when the phone rang
I heard mom say,
"Yes, we still have her"
My stomach lurched,
it cramped; I cried
They came to meet Nessie

As we talked, I was happy Nes was
going to a good home
If we had to sell the farm
at least she would have space to roam
Then there was good news
They invited me to visit

A week later they had me over
Not just to visit
They asked me to train Nessie
So, I go there often
Teaching their little girl to ride
I may not own her, but she is still mine

Darren Lyons

I was never any good in the classroom
until the classroom moved to the shop
There I am a natural
CTE (Career Technical Education)
makes sense for me
I can use this information,
real world skills

When I applied for a job,
they said I had to be eighteen
Waiting isn't my strong suit
This summer I set up my own shop,
took side jobs to earn money
Saved enough pay for tuition
I am going to trade school in the fall

I'll continue my own business
I may not be a scholar, but I am
a leader in my field
FFA president for the school,
state representative
Skills USA competition champion
English grades aren't everything

I can weld a bead that's
smooth, uniform and consistent
draw and read blueprints,
build a product from my own design
I am prepared for whatever
life throws at me
I will forge a path of my own

Juliet Hon

It's not all my fault
Teachers are so unreasonable
How could I meet the project deadline?
I told her I would be on a Hawaiian cruise

It's not like I could reschedule my trip
because she set an arbitrary deadline
I asked for my work before leaving
She said she would help in the morning

I was on a plane in the morning
Nobody can be in two places
at the same time
Unrealistic expectations

I have no idea what to do now
failing that class is not an option
Teachers have too much power
over life and my future

Gloria Oaks

The mirror echoes my smile
My empty eyes stare at my reflection
Why can I see myself, but
nobody else sees me?

If dad would give me back my phone
I could talk to my friends
They live all over the state,
all around the world

He doesn't understand
Says I need to get out, make real friends
He locked me OUT of the house
Who does that?

How did he think that would work?
Did he think people would see me,
and race up to be my friend?
It doesn't work that way

He says my attitude pushes people away
I have friends. He doesn't listen
If he would just give my phone back,
they could soothe my fears

Without their easy contact,
I sit in fear of being
left behind and forgotten
as I look out my bedroom window

John Savoire

That principal lady must pay
She is going to be fined
There wasn't even a fire
She made me walk outside
Ruined my shoes
Dad just bought me new shoes
Now they are ruined

That principal lady must
buy me new shoes
It's her fault
When we came back inside
my shoes were wet
Ruined my new shoes
A thousand-dollar fine

Dad is coming to school
then we'll buy new shoes
She will have to pay for them
I will write a report
They'll have to make her pay
The bell hurt my ears
I want to go home

Eduardo Fitzgerald

Everyone thinks I'm older
I'm only 17, graduating next year
They threaten that I won't
I walk close to the cliff, but
I won't fall and jeopardize my future
Life's a balancing act
like walking a tight rope

My full beard creates
the illusion that I am an adult
Makes me the beer runner
Gets me accepted by the right crowd
Most kids keep their distance
In this neighborhood, my people are
troublemakers to avoid

The English teacher
wanted me to attend study hall
No way! I can do the work.
I ain't stupid. He's a dick
Mom says it will hurt my self-esteem
I don't have to go
School already is bad enough

Everyone is always out to get us
Racists
Dark skin translates to terrorist
Tempers really flared when they threatened to
put my rottweilers down
Hell, no! That won't happen

Those damn cats were in our yard
The neighbors say we owe them 3,000 dollars
Dad had to pay a ticket in court
Nobody can tell us what to do
I am just like my dogs
protecting our turf

RJ Ellis

It all started when I was a kid
Dad went to prison
I wasn't upset; I didn't feel anything
Nothing really hurt
I remember punching a wall
Didn't notice my hand was bleeding
until some kid mentioned it

They say I have anger problems
Want me to talk to someone,
but I don't see it as a problem
A problem is something
that needs to be fixed
My anger is a support
It helps manage life

Long story short

They have a plan for me at school
Search my backpack when I enter the building
Redirect when I show signs of escalation
like when I growl and make heavy sighs
they change the activity
They think they are controlling me but
I control their reactions

You should see them when I belch and fart

If I get really agitated
and don't calm after a timeout,
they shove me into a padded room
but not until I take off my
belt and shoes
Guess they're afraid I'll hang myself
It's not me I want to hurt

Social Worker
School Resource Officer
Probation
Cops
Man, I can make them all dance

Dad's getting out of prison next month
He will be proud
that I am following in his footsteps

Kyle Wheeler

Everything was rainbows and lollipops
Then, it went to shit
We sat
eating popcorn
watching a movie
Dogs were barking
I got off my lazy ass,
walked to the window
The moon was bright
They stood in the street
yelling back and forth
It was a big shit show
in front of the neighbors
pitching things
kicking the car
I sent my little sister
to the closet,
dialed 911
Mom and Dad
intoxicated
But when the cops came,
Mom wigged out
cussed at them,
threw a beer bottle
They cuffed her
I recall a hand on her head
She ducked into the back seat
Dad's eyes went hollow
Maybe, my call was wrong
The result was my fault
I block my sorrow
My heart is empty
Music makes an artificial beat
Anger is redirected
When all else fails
A good fist fight offers focus
creates a reason to hurt
that I can deal with

Carmen Haines

I do not like science
It is a conundrum
Why give the right answers
if they will be marked wrong?
They won't allow me
to share the truth
God created the world

Mom expects better grades
She says the teacher will help me
They created a system
When I hold up my hand
touch my finger to my thumb
it signals my discomfort
The lesson invalidates my beliefs
so I leave the room

How does this help?
With a fable for a text,
my grade is still a D
They lack evidence
A diagram misrepresents
illustrates their realities
disperses disinformation
followed by worksheets and tests

Do I honor my mother
by earning respectable grades?
Appease a secular world?
Should I taste perjury?

Maya Griggs

The end of the year is the hardest
It's a lot of work to earn decent grades
Procrastination's my worst bad habit
I must juggle
sports, school
family, friends
Grades are the first to suffer
Social time is needed to balance life

Often, I'm sleep deprived
Sleep's overrated
When I am late for school,
Mom calls in to excuse me
She understands
The school doesn't get my situation
They record a tardy or an absence
if it's more than 30 minutes

Even my grandma called the office
She was fuming that they wouldn't
excuse the absence when I helped her move
No way, no how am I losing credit
Then my parents got mad at me!
They took away privileges
Like it's my fault!
High school is unreasonable

Chloe Walter

I look around at the purple walls
It's a comfortable place
This is my last time at this locker
in this hallway, with these faces
Who decided purple is a good school color?

At least I will finish the year before moving
School's the only constant in my life
The ringing bells bring relief
They're consistent, dependable, familiar
These buildings provide comfort

During my ten years of school,
I've attended thirteen schools
I don't miss individuals, never have
Can't say I have friends, just acquaintances
Never known anyone long enough

Each time it gets harder,
harder to try
I'm often alone
In grade school,
I sat against the brick wall

Here,
I lean against the bricks trying to blend in
or at least not stand out - that's worse

Sports aren't usually an option because
I enroll mid-season
I quit joining the teams,
the clubs, the groups
Too much regret

With no one to talk to, I read
Books take me to new worlds,
comfortable places
I stop feeling the awkwardness
of not fitting in

In a book, I become a character
join the adventures
connect to the town's people
develop an identity
participate

I wonder what waits in Galveston

Chris Uyeda

I've known people who love to eat
for that matter I love food
Overtime people gain weight
Dad's paunch hangs over his belt
more this year than last
We call it his spare tire and laugh
I've never known anybody
to slowly dissolve for lack of food
That's what I witness with my sister
She is fading away
We all press her to eat while
assuming it is a teenage girl phase

At dinner she scoops food onto her plate,
but the amount decreases daily
If I wasn't paying attention,
I might not have noticed
the portions shrink in size
Stealthily,
she pushes the morsels around
mixing, then spreading them apart
Making it seem like she is eating

A master at not eating
Nobody noticed at first
Then everybody saw
what was right before our eyes

She was admitted to the hospital
Hooked up to a feeding tube

That's when the shit got real!

Sara Uyeda

They say I am a strong lady
I don't feel strong
just tired
It hurts to move,
stand,
breathe,
live
It hurts to have no choices

I lay in bed
while a tube pumps food
sustaining my body
I guess I had a choice
to live or die
but, to be alive
I had to resign myself to this,
a disease that won't let me thrive

Week after week,
progress is slow
Food is reintroduced
constantly monitoring for
reactions that might
reject the healing process
Wary that any change
might end what has begun

At school I am told,
"Make friends.
Learn to live"
No one should have to learn to live
It is simply something we do
like breathing
But then I can't do that without thinking
and hurting

David Walker

Anger is my enemy
Can't believe I tamed it
As a freshman I thought
it would devour me
It fed off my failures

Anxiety
amped up comes out as anger
As assignments got longer and harder,
my mind become confused – jumbled
School is a puzzle with no straight edges

Negative thoughts made me
think I couldn't control reality
Like a self-fulfilling prophesy
my chest tightened, and I was
set up for failure, ready to accept it

When I learned to think positively,
it was like trading in my body
for a new, upgraded model with
warning lights and
sensors that signal danger

This new version of me
knows when to breathe slowly,
put the brakes on illogical thinking,
swerve around the potholes,
open up to new possibilities

Mandy Fowers

Thank goodness Brandon will graduate
I am so tired of being compared to him
I can't even begin to compete
and why would I want to
He's my brother

When he walks into the room,
girls' heads turn
boys gravitate to him to be validated
If you are friends with Brandon,
you are somebody

But I am his sister. I am nobody
except Brandon's little sister
Sometimes I think my name is
Brandon's Little Sister,
my shallow claim to fame

People do not sit in anticipation
waiting for the punch line or
to see what I will do next
I am virtually unknown
This year

Brandon Fowers

I will walk to get my diploma
knowing there's a new road to travel
But I have no idea where I am going
Who thought it would be this terrifying?

Mandy always looks at me with admiration
She believes all the friends, awards, praise
mean I have it all figured out. When in fact,
I don't even know what I need to figure out

She once said she envies me
Wouldn't she be surprised, I am jealous of her
She is an original, one of a kind
I only understand how to play the crowd

I become whoever and whatever
they want me to be
But after high school when they are gone,
who will I be?

Sis, she's true to herself
knows what she wants
A self-made success story
She's going somewhere

Brynn Lawson

Well – I am still here
Never thought I'd survive
the debt, departure,
divorce, depression

Each took a little piece of me
When dad lost his job
I thought it was only money until
everything started to disappear

Moving was tolerable
I remember thinking it's just
a wood structure. Then I realized,
home is more than building supplies

Friends left, and new ones came
Everything was replaceable
until Mom moved out
taking my heart but not me

Leaving a cool darkness
like she packed away the laughter
the smiles, the traditions,
everything that lighted my existence

I simply didn't care
I shrugged and quit
It wasn't until they named
the apathy that controlled me

Depressive disorder
It's treatable and slowly
my world brightened
like moving the dimmer switch

Morgan Tilman

When the school year started,
the dog days of summer were
fading and the prospects of fall
energized the reality of school

For years we had a solid routine
My dog walked my brother and me
to the bus stop. Once we boarded,
Mom locked him in the house

But this year the routine changed
because I was in high school
It didn't seem like a big deal, but then
we don't recognize death at our doorstep

On the first day of school,
Titus walked me to the bus stop
then, I watched him return to the house
through the open door

When Sammy walked to his bus,
he was escorted by Mom and our
vigorous pup. As the bus approached,
Mom locked him in the car

Titus' internal clock alerted him
each day when I stepped off the bus
He stood at the end of the driveway waiting
wagging his tail. But not that day

He wasn't inside the door or on my bed
He didn't come when I called
Mom said she hadn't seen him since . . .
She started to cry and ran outside

When I opened the car door there was silence
Titus was laying in the back seat – lifeless
Mom ran beside me, held my hand and wept
I lifted his body and laid him on the grass

Kameron Wordal

With the filling of the prescription,
I feel calmer, more in control
I don't know what they're afraid of
I never wanted to hurt anyone
a restraining order is a little overkill

I swear, I follow the script
but the bottle is always
closer to empty than full
I thought the Dr. messed up,
but I counted them
One-a-day for thirty days
They were all there
at the beginning of the month

Dad tries to be supportive but
if he misses anymore work,
he won't have a job to return to
I don't know how he does it

He takes care of all eight of us,
me and the five younger ones
My problems alone cause stress
Now Melissa's pregnant. She's 16
That'll add another mouth to feed

Dad always steps up
Mom's no easy task
He makes sure she gets to AA
As long as she makes the meeting,
things aren't too bad
You know the saying,
"If Mama ain't happy,
Ain't nobody happy"

Lately, she's been happy
Lives in a cloud or floats on top
Hope I can stay out of trouble
If only my meds lasted the month

Harrison Paxton

The night leaves a powdery landscape
waiting to be invaded and awakened
My sled purrs as it warms up contrasting
the silent shivering of my frozen core
Both spewing vapor from the condensation

Snow floats and wipes the windshield
The skis floating over the once unmarked
snow provides a confidence only shared
after successfully highmarking a peak,
when the adrenaline is also at its highest

Sweat dampens the layers protecting
against the icy, cold environment
Late season creates a hard snow but,
we say a bad day on a machine is better
than the best day at school

Gaps in trees beckon as loudly as they warn
Sun beams invite us to the meadow
We enter the solitude leaving behind
evidence of boondocking and side hilling
messed up with jumps and drops

At the high-altitude I reach white peaks
remove helmet, googles, and gloves
knowing the season's ending, and I must
survive on the fumes of memories
until it snows again

Aidan Farooq

As each year progresses,
I have a thought, no a question
Where are my friends?
I sit at lunch eating alone

In an overcrowded high school,
pals are hard to find
Faces are intimidating even when
they smile and say kind words

Mr. Case, the counselor, enrolled
me in a lunch friendship group
An invitation he said,
but it doesn't feel like I have a choice

Over time, the group started to hang
Choosing to spend time together
beyond the scheduled lunch periods
Someone used the word friendship

Jesus Aquilar

I don't know where to begin
How to fix my problem
The cause is a mystery, and
I have no idea who can help

I always lose homework
Teachers are annoyed
They call my parents
who then become angry

Everyone knows it is a problem
but nobody can solve it
They ask why?
I donno
When?
I shrug

Tempers rise as do voices
Adults send me to my room,
a place that provides comfort
Nobody yells at me or looks upset
I want to start my homework
but never remember what to do
or how to do it

Then the counselor provides
A name for my challenge,
disorganized distress
He provides a simple solution,
a system of binders with dividers,
structured sanity

Isaiah Skow

Elementary school was the beginning
I remember
The first time the teacher asked,
"Where's your homework?"
I responded,
"I don't know."
She looked disappointed
I would have liked it better if she'd
just been mad
That came later
But how could I answer the question?
    "Where is it?"
    "Where is something if it doesn't exist?"
So, I started lying.
    "It's at home."
    "On my bed."
    "Lost it on the bus."
    "I can't find it."
The disappointment shifted to anger
which was easier
but nothing good comes from anger
so, I ignored it
Pretty soon the teacher ignored
my missing work
Then she ignored me

It was easier for us both
Figures

Kenneth Smith

Shyness is an illness
I don't care what they say
Nike's "Just Do It" slogan
can't cure my distress
It's not that simple
Thanks to my school counselor,
I met some kids I call friends

The first time I met with him
it was frightening
A pass was handed to me to report to the office
I'd never been in trouble before
so, standing up in the middle of class,
walking out of World Civ
felt paralyzing

When I entered the office,
he greeted me with a smile,
escorted me to a quiet place,
shut the door. When we were seated
he said, "I notice you sit alone at lunch."

I nodded.
"Why is that?
I didn't want to seem disrespectful,
but I shrugged thinking,
"I don't know anyone. Nobody knows me."
I looked at the tile floor

My stomach hurt
At my lack of words, he asked,
"May I introduce you to some boys?"
I couldn't say no. I didn't say anything
Just sat reluctantly interested
The next day I met Isiah, Aidan and Jesus
I am transformed like in a movie
but not into a large robot

Erica Quintana

No one needs to know – not now
I even try to forget
since we moved to town
I'll have the chance to start over

Mom loves me in her own way
but just saying, "I love you"
doesn't make my heart all gooey
in fact, just the opposite

Her actions make me cold
I've been frozen to the bone
ever since we moved to this town
Why'd Dad pick such a cold place?

Once Mom gets out of jail,
our visits must be supervised
by a court appointed adult
No way Dad will do that

His feelings are perfectly clear
He did and does hate her
Says she put us through hell
Unforgivable

My counselor says to respect myself
So, I made the decision to cut ties
Mom expects me to welcome her
with open arms when she's released

Our move will ease the separation
unless I contact Mom,
she won't know where we are
All I'm required to do is go to school

Dress normal, act nice,
do my work, and if I do cry
it's not because I made the wrong decision
It's because sometimes - only sometimes I miss her

Melissa Stika

Sam's been a friend since second grade
That's half my life
Megan started hanging with us last year
Kelly joined our group in August

Kelly is like the moon in the eclipse
When she steps into my circle,
I fade away
Stories of our past bond the group

We talked about trips to the cabin,
walks in the streams,
hikes in the mountains,
roasting marshmallows, swimming

We laughed at everything
Now, laughter is not cool
The cabin is uncool
My stories are boring

It not what Kelly says
It's what she doesn't say
The way she scrunches her nose,
rolls her eyes

Lately,
I've been wondering,
Can a friend be a
Bully?

Samantha Melendez

Melissa and I have always been friends
but I want to have other friends too

Kelly may be new to our group
but she is still a friend

Why should I have to choose?
This drama stresses me to the max

Sometimes, I just wanna
go home, turn off my phone, and sleep

I don't understand this friendship stuff
I earn a 4.0 without cracking a book – easy
Making and keeping friends is hard

Megan Maas

Life feels like a soap opera
spinning out of control
While laying on my bed
with my head under the blankets
I feel secure

When standing on my feet,
the spinning keeps me unbalanced
Questioning,
        Are they laughing at me?
Wondering,
        Am I pretty enough?
Wishing,
        Just wishing
These are the days of my life

Everyone thinks the world
revolves around them, or should
If one person disappears,
the world keeps rotating
Life continues as the world turns

When I joined art club,
girls welcomed me without questions
The past wasn't discussed
They are my present
Their gravity grounds me
The here is now
It does not predict the future
The world is not flat

Kelly Rey

What is her problem?
I said, "I'm sorry."
She shouldn't have read my post
Anyway, I wasn't talking to her
and biotch is just slang
It doesn't mean anything
Melissa doesn't like sharing attention
She thinks she's a queen,
queen of the mountain
Maybe, when she's at her cabin

People ought to know
words hurt
Mia and Diane are mean
They'll get what they deserve
thinking they're all that
I don't require their devotion
Let them throw a pity party
'cause I am hanging with
Sam and Megan
Oh, and Queen Melissa

Diane Sabin

Since middle school, Mia's been my friend
Pro'bly 'cause our names are alphabetical
Sabin – Saki
A coincidence?
No way! I believe in fate

When I ran to my dad's
the only reason they found me was
Kelly's restless lip syndrome
If she can't be trusted,
then we can't be friends

The SRO found us in the bathroom
We weren't skipping biology
just needed time to talk
Kelly told where we were
Wonder if there's a cure
to seal those lips

Mia Saki

"I know, right?!"
It was a mistake
That's what caused the problem
I only meant to send it to Diane
but accidentally wrote in it a group message

It's true so it can't be gossip
Kelly can't be trusted with secrets
When she started to cry,
I told her to not take it the wrong way
I said, "No offense"

She makes everything so personal
when it doesn't have to be a big deal

Olivia Harper

Last time going to my school
Last time walking to class with Corinne
Last time playing on the team

When I wave goodbye,
our vacant house may look the same
It will no longer be home

Grief overcomes me
Denial
I tell them I am not going
Anger
We don't talk anymore
Bargain
I plead to stay
Depression
A sadness envelops me

Until something connects,
nightmares develop into dreams
I wake in my bed
feeling comfortable

Eventually,
days provide some light
Eventually,
I agree to try
Finally,
I become part of the change
Suddenly,
my journey ends
I feel a peace
Acceptance

Matthew Simpson

I am glad it's over
One hell of a year but I'll graduate,
no thanks to my old man
He blames everything on me

He doesn't congratulate me
even though I kicked the habit
He won't even discuss my
past drug use – just judges

"You reap what you sew,"
he says as he walks past me
I never hear well done or
I am proud of you, Son

I passed four English classes
Four in one year!
I remember a time Dad said
he'd always support me

When I walk across that stage,
they'll hand me a diploma
I'll know I succeeded
I achieved this for myself

Corinne Simpson

Ever since that phone woke us up at midnight,
my family has been cleaning up his messes
He doesn't realize the damage he's done
Financially, emotionally, I don't trust him,
my big brother
He is supposed to be my role model

When I was little, I admired him
wanted to be just like Matthew
Followed him around like a lost puppy
Now, I try to hide that we're related
n embarrassment,
a blemish on the family name

The last straw was the party
at our house while we were on vacation
We planned to visit Washington, DC,
see the sights and enjoy the history
Instead, the phone rang,
police busted a party at our house

Now, Matt is planning to graduate
He expects us to cheer and be proud
Says he has made a new start; he's clean,
but we've heard all that before
Pathological
Personally, I won't trust him ever again

I am glad he is graduating
He'll move out, provide my family
peace, stop the constant worrying
He makes me feel like I am riding a
Merry-go-round
and I, for one, am ready to get off

AnnaBell Carson

Living in Germany for the summer
is a dream come true
Frau Hannah promises my host family is perfect

Coming from a family of nine
the challenge will be learning
to be more than a number

As the oldest child,
I am already a live-in nanny

My host family has no children
They love hosting students,
short term visitors from other countries

Their names are Adel and Tab
I googled their meanings: brave and brilliant
The bravest thing I've ever done is board the plane
I haven't done that yet

Mrs. Smith - Vice Principal

Like a child's birthday party, the last day of school
comes complete with decorations and music
When the sounds of excitement reach an apex,
the final bell releases students to float away
Reminiscent of fugitive balloons

As the celebration ends, the multi-colored forms
following the laws of nature
drift, hover, soar towards the exits
Contingent upon the amount of air and
speed expelled at their liberation

Some when pricked by the awareness of freedom
jump, run and spiral towards the doors
Only slowing to bump a peer with a high five
Excited to leave behind the expectations and
rules that have tied them down

Others slowly, unconsciously wander
as they leave behind the structure and security
offered by teachers, nurses, counselors, coaches
Deflated in the knowledge that daily
supports are now inaccessible

The taste of a half-eaten birthday cake
hangs in the halls; the sweetness has dissolved
leaving crumbs of the unwanted or forgotten
The building begins to sag, grows hollow
and sinks in upon itself

The defects of scuffed floors, carved desks,
stained ceilings remind that without the
students, this is an abandoned vestibule
Silent until the fall when students' laughter
and apprehension greet another homecoming

Author's Commentary

During a conversation with my father who was 85 at the time, he asserted the issues teens face today are no worse than when he was a kid. I disagreed. We found consensus that problems have existed for every generation. The dialogue required me to reexamine my premise, the problems of our world negatively impact hope for the future.

Youth hear a mantra encouraging them to make a difference, and many seize opportunities to positively impact the world. They inspire and remind me of the power of optimism. Unfortunately, based on 34 years in public education and 60 years of life, I fear today's teens live in apathy, leaving them lethargic and indifferent because they believe the future is spiraling downward out of control.

In her One Voice Special (1986) Barbra Streisand pointed to the past as inspiration for the future.

> ". . . But I have great faith in people. I believe if they're told, if they know what's at stake, they will make a change. They always have. Whether it was the civil rights movement, the woman's movement, or the Vietnam War. When the clear voice of the people is heard, it has always changed the course of history . . . Sometimes we forget the importance of one voice, of each of our voices."

Our faith in the future is at stake. If we combine our voices to advance healthy practices, optimism can replace apathy.

"Everything that is done in this world is done by hope."
— Martin Luther

My granddaughter, an academically advanced seventh grade student, shared her anxiety during overstimulating, overcrowded school experiences. We discussed incidents from the last year where her hands started to shake, her stomach churned, and her head ached. Once, she made an excuse to go to the bathroom where she cried in the stall. During normal everyday situations, she felt out of control; there were no immediate dangers or threats simply uncertainty and apprehension.

Coretta Scott King sounded a warning bell.

"The failure to invest in youth reflects a lack of compassion and a colossal failure of common sense."

If one voice can accomplish so much, think of the possibilities if the nation chimes together. Youth are America's most valuable commodity. The time is appropriate to revisit an old axiom, "Many hands make light work." Or to apply a more modern cliché, "It takes a village to raise a child."

Examining the problem from different lenses

Problems are multifaceted, and sustainable change requires input from all stakeholders. The ideas of citizens who view the world through different lenses provide perspective to understand various concerns.

Parents and guardians feel uncomfortable entering the school. Their feelings are based on negative interactions from past experiences, limited knowledge about school procedures, and doubts about their academic skills, not to mention, most children do not want parents to invade their space.

Teachers welcome support in the classrooms but raise questions about how to find time to train volunteers, address child privacy laws, security, and logistically how to add additional bodies to an already overcrowded environment.

The teachers who dedicate hours beyond the regular workday, the parents who struggle to manage limited time, the legislatures who strive to address the concern of constituents, everybody and every group has honest intentions. No clear answers appear. Instead of one grand choir small fractions plan in isolation. Seldom, if ever, do we set aside our agendas to compose a harmonious, melodious, congruous plan of action. Change is difficult. Maybe getting all the stakeholders in the same room is a pie in the sky idea. Instead, consider what unites individuals in a common goal.

Think about the events that garner audience attention: Superbowls, World Series, Academy Awards. Shouldn't our children rank as high as sporting events and entertainment? There is no quick answer, but we can impact positive change by modeling positive life behaviors. Everyone has the opportunity, the responsibility, to model constructive conduct that builds empathy and eliminates apathy.

"I think the biggest problem in the world is that we have a generation of young people, and maybe two, who don't think it's going to get any better." – John Denver

Five values shape responsible, empathetic youth

My childhood, like everyone's, had difficulties. Life is not perfect. However, my parents lived according to five values that shaped who I am today. These are the same five values I attempt to model for students in the classroom and with my family at home: security, work ethic, discipline, respect, and education.

Security

I recognize my fortune growing up in a middle-class home in the 70's. An adult greeted us when we walked into the house after school. We ate together at the dinner table and talked about our day. Security may not look the same in each home but exists when a child knows what to expect. Don't get me wrong, we were certainly not a family of perfection. My parents argued but hurled words, not fists.

Kids played outside during all seasons without concerns about global warming. In the spring, irrigation ditches became the public swimming pools, and nobody feared pesticides. When it was time to come home for the night, dad's whistle echoed around the block.

Summers produced red cherries, green apples, scraped knees and opportunities to sleep outside. I question if sunscreen or mosquito spray existed. Fall brought cooler weather and Halloween. Dressed in costumes sewn by mom, we trick-or-treated. At home, we devoured candy and handmade treats without even thinking about having them x-rayed.

Work Ethic

Children accept what they witness. My parents accepted work as mandatory to survival. They never expected others to support our family. They demonstrated the correlation between work and success.

With money a limited resource, we built stilts out of extra 2 X 6 boards, and dad made us wooden guns that shot rubber strips cut from old bike tubes. We knew not to aim at anyone, and nobody ever lost an eye.

We played with our neighbors and getting together meant gathering in the backyard. As a teen when I wanted money to go to a movie, I gathered aluminum cans to recycle, babysat, or pulled weeds. Work provided opportunities. I never saw anyone sitting outside the grocery store with a sign asking for money.

Discipline

When a problem arose in our neighborhood, parents met and shared concerns on the front doorstep. A resolution developed with input from all parties without placing blame or shirking responsibility.

Adults actively participated in children's lives. The options to keep secrets were limited because a cord attached phones to the wall and conversations occurred in the kitchen within hearing range of the family.

Respect

We were normal kids who made mistakes and accepted consequences. Insolence was not tolerated, especially towards mom. "Wait until your father gets home," produced repentance.

In return, adults respected our ideas. We had family night once a week where we played games and discussed issues. TV shows presented families like ours. Our lives were reality, not something to measure against reality TV.

In the winter, when it snowed, we built forts, launched sleds, and a day ended with hot chocolate topped with marshmallows. We said Merry Christmas and accepted both Santa and Christ into our homes.

Individuals maintained personal viewpoints, disagreements occurred, but people listened and shook hands when they parted. Citizens addressed the president with civility; audiences stood for the Pledge of Allegiance, and the American flag represented honor.

Education

All our friends attended public school. The curriculum consisted of reading, writing, math, science, and values. Church preached creationism while science teachers explained evolution. Nobody complained.

If we got in trouble at school, we understood the punishment at home would be twice as harsh. Drugs and alcohol were unseen at school, nobody vaped, and school shootings didn't exist.

When I graduated, I enrolled in college because I desired a higher education and paid tuition by working. The responsibility to choose the direction of my life rested with me but was supported by important adults.

A solution for consideration

Disagreements about the causes of societal problems may never be resolved; in fact, whether a problem exists is still up for debate. However, the perception is real: increased anxiety, depression, violence, suicide, and bullying.

So, let's return to the problem of how to create change in our world. What if every member of society sang the same tune? What if the refrain consisted of five themes: security, work ethic, discipline, respect, and education? If everyone modeled similar values, as a society, we could build a stable world for youth to grow and mature, a place where we all sing in unity to produce optimism.

The responsibility rests neither with us to pass a perfect world on to the next generation nor to expect them to solve all the world's problems. Instead, it is our civic responsibility to build and model a lifestyle that exhibits behaviors that promote change, establishes a vision of a productive society, encourages invention and creative solutions, and demands work to build a world where everyone can exist and define their reality.

Youth can change the world. It is time we reveal the power they hold in their hands and model a path to build a prosperous future.

About the Author

Brenda Mahler is a retired educator with 34 years' experience. As an English teacher and administrator, she learned about life from her students while walking the halls. She carries the memories of the lives of the students who taught her compassion, the value of overcoming challenges and the need to compromise. Her passion for teaching grew each year as she realized the power of one person to make a difference in the lives of others. *Lockers Speak* allows the voices of youth from her past to speak their truths.

As a wife, mother and grandmother, Brenda continues to write about life experiences acknowledging that everyday holds opportunities to learn, grow, and inspire. Her writing can be enjoyed on multiple websites. Join the 3K+ readers who follow her by visiting anyone of the many sites where she publishes.

- I AM My Best!, iammybest.org, her personal blog
- Medium's digital magazine where she enjoys top writer status and is editor of multiple publications
- Vocal Media where her stories have repeatedly earned Top Story status
- Manystories, a platform that often features her articles

Made in the USA
Monee, IL
27 May 2023

34762122R00098